Maybe having Mr. Irresistible right next door wasn't such a great idea... but it sure made her feel safe.

Physically safe, that is. All bets were off when it came to her emotional safety.

"I'll be fine. We do not need to leave the door open."

"I'll settle for unlocked."

"Fine. I'll leave the door unlocked, but I promise you won't need to come rushing to my rescue in the middle of the night."

In two long strides Matt stood in front of her, taking her breath away with his nearness, his masculine scent, the dark bristles sprinkled across his chin...and the look in his dark eyes. "I won't mind if I have to."

CAROL ERICSON

INTUITION

HARLEQUIN®
entertain, enrich, inspire™

To the baristas of the Palos Verdes Starbucks.

ISBN-13: 978-0-373-74694-1

INTUITION

Copyright © 2012 by Carol Ericson

Recycling programs for this product may not exist in your area.

www.Harlequin.com

Printed in U.S.A.

ABOUT THE AUTHOR

Carol Ericson lives with her husband and two sons in Southern California, home of state-of-the-art cosmetic surgery, wild freeway chases, palm trees bending in the Santa Ana winds and a million amazing stories. These stories, along with hordes of virile men and feisty women, clamor for release from Carol's head. It makes for some interesting headaches until she sets them free to fulfill their destinies and her readers' fantasies. To find out more about Carol, her books and her strange headaches, please visit her website, www.carolericson.com, "where romance flirts with danger."

Books by Carol Ericson

CAST OF CHARACTERS

Matt Conner—A former cop turned private investigator, Matt's not too thrilled when he finds out he has to share his first case as a P.I. with a psychic—even if that psychic turns out to be Kylie Grant, the sexiest soothsayer in town.

Kylie Grant—She returns to her hometown to bring hope or closure to a grieving family whose daughter disappeared three years ago. Instead, she finds her high school crush all grown up and meddling with her ability to do her job.

Bree Harris—The disappearance of this young woman three years ago brings both Kylie and Matt back to Coral Cove. Kylie is determined to bring closure to Bree's parents, or die trying.

Harlan Sloan—This wheeling, dealing concert promoter enjoys the perks of his job: plenty of willing young women to ease his lonely nights. But did the fun and games end in tragedy when one young woman tried to get too close?

Eric Evans—The police chief's son leads a charmed life. He was friendly with Bree, but his father's investigation of her disappearance never managed to investigate that friendship too closely.

Police Chief Evans—He was the chief of police when Bree went missing. Now he doesn't appreciate Matt and Kylie questioning his judgment...or his son.

Toby Reynolds—A local man, he enjoys working as a roadie for Coral Cove's music festival. He knew and liked Bree and is more than willing to assist Kylie with her investigation, but is he too willing?

Mindy Lawrence—She was friendly with Bree and was one of the last people to see her before she disappeared, but her cryptic notes about Bree to Matt and Kylie make her a person of interest.

Mayor Tyler Davis—The mayor of Coral Cove, he's not at all happy that Kylie and Matt are dredging up a distasteful event in Coral Cove's past. But he may have other reasons for keeping a lid on Bree's disappearance from the music festival.

Chapter One

Her mother's body dangled before her like a life-size puppet waiting for some puppet master to pull the strings and give her life. But that wasn't going to happen.

Kylie Grant's mouth yawned open in a silent scream as her mother's body swooped toward her. The head of the puppet jerked upright, and the eyes clicked open.

You should have known. You should have known.

Kylie struggled to wrench her gaze away from the accusing figure before her. If she looked away, it would disappear. If she looked away, she would awaken from her nightmare. If she looked away, she would never get the answers she needed.

Kylie managed a strangled cry as she bolted upright in the hotel bed. A cold sweat claimed her flesh, and she shivered.

Now. She had to make a move now.

Tumbling out of the bed, she squinted at the lighted green digits of the alarm clock. Not exactly witching hour, but late enough for her to slip into Columbella House unnoticed while the tourists wined and dined.

She splashed some cold water on her face, stuffed her feet into her sandals and grabbed her purse from the back of the chair. She didn't need anything else. All the tools she required resided in her head.

She slipped out of her hotel room and punched the call button for the elevator. After a brief journey for three floors, the doors opened onto the lobby.

Kylie flew out of the elevator, bumping shoulders with a tall, broad man entering the car.

She glanced up, way up. "Excuse me."

The man ducked his head, but Kylie spun on her heel and raced toward the lobby before he could respond.

A flash of recognition pierced her brain. Matt, the town bad boy and all-around troublemaker from her high school class. She should've figured she'd run into some former classmates when she returned to Coral Cove. Too bad the first one had to be someone she particularly despised. Rock 'n' roll playing, motorcycle riding, black jeans wearing Matt…Matt Conner.

Kylie breezed through the lobby and shoved open the front doors. The cool night air hit her face and she put all thoughts of former classmates, even gorgeous ones like Matt Conner, out of her head. She was on a mission and the timing couldn't be better.

The restaurants of Coral Cove's Main Street teemed with activity, tourists home from the beach and all cleaned up, rubbed elbows with the locals home from work. Kylie's stomach rumbled. She'd eaten a late lunch and then zonked out in her hotel room. She could use a snack, but Columbella House called and she was ready to answer its demand.

After a short drive on the Coast Highway, Kylie turned onto Coral Cove Drive and rolled to a stop at the curb that fronted the abandoned Victorian. She grabbed the flashlight from the seat next to her and slipped out of the car.

She eased open the side gate, holding her breath as it squeaked a protest. It wasn't as though anyone would hear her approach. The house had been empty for years. She blew out the trapped breath and followed the path to the side of the house, her sandals crunching on the sand beneath her feet.

The beam of her flashlight played across the side door to the kitchen, a piece of warped plywood in place of the window. Rumor had it that anyone could get into Columbella through this side door...or the secret door from the beach if one knew how to reach it. Kylie knew about the beach access, but she'd have to come up to the house through the basement and, well…she wasn't going near that basement.

She peeled back the plywood and unlocked the door from the inside. Stepping into the kitchen, she aimed her flashlight into the hallway. Her feet moved in the direction of the light, ready or not.

Kylie shuffled into the hallway and placed her flashlight on a dusty credenza. She gazed up at the third-floor landing where her mother's body had once hung. Clutching her upper arms, she shivered.

"Mom?" The whisper escaped her lips like a sigh.

Columbella House seemed to close around her, wrapping her in a clammy embrace, inviting her to stay awhile. She swallowed and straightened her spine, brushing off the macabre welcome. She had no intention of succumbing to the house's gloomy atmosphere.

Just as she had no intention of succumbing to the same demons that had dogged her mother—not that Kylie didn't have the same demons. The horrors of her particular gift visited her with alarming frequency, but she'd been able to whip them into shape, bend them to her own will and make them dance to her own tune. The clichés that tumbled through her mind allowed her to impose a sense of normalcy on her powers.

She turned from the stairs, not ready to confront

what awaited her on the landing. She snatched her flashlight from the table, and the dust particles gleamed in the beam of light. She aimed the light at the basement door, and goose bumps trickled across her flesh all over again.

One of these days, she'd make her way down to the basement of Columbella and test out the strength of her gift, but not now. Not tonight. She had a mission.

Actually, she had two missions in Coral Cove this summer, but the personal one took precedence on this particular night. It was no coincidence that the job she'd signed on to do in Coral Cove coincided with the anniversary of her mother's suicide.

Kylie didn't believe in coincidences. She wandered into the library. Remnants from the police investigation into the two deaths that occurred in this room remained—strings outlining the dead bodies' positions and chalk markings from the spent bullet casings. But these were recent bodies…just two more in the continuing parade of death that marched through this house.

At least in the case of these two deaths, the good guys had prevailed. Hometown boy turned war hero, Kieran Roarke, had taken out a couple of killers who'd had their sights on a little boy, his boy. Maybe Columbella's reputation was changing.

Her gaze tracked to the burnt-out room tucked

off the back wall of the library. Another case of good triumphing over evil. Another Roarke, Colin this time, had rescued Michelle Girard from a crazed serial killer—a crazed serial killer who'd happened to be Kylie's high school algebra teacher. No wonder she hated math.

Her fingertips buzzed as she trailed them along the scorched walls. She was in a state of heightened sensitivity. She'd known it from the moment she'd rolled out of bed after her nightmare. That's what had led her to this house tonight.

Of course, she should be using her heightened awareness to get down to business and do the job that Mrs. Harris had hired her to do. But she owed it to her mother to investigate her suicide. She'd been too traumatized to do it before.

Since returning to Coral Cove a few days ago for the Harris job, she'd been waiting for the right time to visit Columbella House. Nobody *visited* Columbella these days. People came here to explore, to rendezvous, to hide, to investigate. To confront old ghosts.

So maybe she should get busy.

She rubbed the soot from her fingers on the seat of her jeans, and drew in a deep breath. She couldn't waste this opportunity. She'd already wasted three years.

She crept back to the staircase and put a tentative foot on the first step. It squeaked. With her hand skimming the carved wood banister, she jogged up the remaining steps to the second-floor landing. One more floor to go.

When she hit the top step of the third floor, she dug into her purse and withdrew the necklace Mom had always worn—up to and including the day she killed herself.

Clutching the necklace in one clammy hand, Kylie set the flashlight on the scarred wood floor, pointing the beam of light at the ceiling. Her purse slid from her shoulder, and she let it drop to the floor next to the flashlight.

She took two steps forward and tripped to a stop. She'd been plotting and planning this moment for so long, her reluctance surprised her. Not that she ever believed it would be easy. That's why it had taken so long for her to get around to it.

Gripping the balustrade, she shuffled toward The Spot. How long had it taken Mom to climb those stairs? Had she done it with fear? Confidence? Desperation?

Time to find out.

Kylie faced the house. Creating two white-knuckled fists, her hands curled around the railing, crushing the chain of the necklace against her palm. She closed her eyes and filled her lungs with the musty, sea-dampened air that permeated the house.

Breathing deeply, she rolled back her shoulders

and loosened her grip. She had to let down the guard she'd perfected over the years. Topple the barriers her mother had taught her to erect, barriers Mom wasn't strong enough to maintain herself.

Kylie allowed the sensations that had been hovering on the brink of her consciousness all day to take over. She took another deep breath through her nose and sidled to the left a few steps—right to the place where Mom had slipped the noose over her head and jumped.

She gulped around the lump in her throat. "Why, Mom?"

A gush of cool air swirled past her, and she hunched her shoulders. With her senses on high alert and her mind an open portal, all manner of otherworldly phenomena had access to her very being. But she wanted to focus on just one tragedy of the past. She let the others roll across her mind and body, filtering with every ounce of her will, squeezing the necklace in her hand so hard, the imprint of the chain burned into her skin.

A jolt of terror stabbed her chest, and her body bucked. Fear so strong she could sense the metallic aftertaste in her mouth swept through her limbs, weakening her knees. She sagged against the railing.

"Were you afraid before you did it, Mom?"

A cold presence pressed against Kylie's back,

forcing her against the railing. She couldn't open her eyes, couldn't turn around…couldn't breathe.

She sifted through the images and messages cascading through her brain. She scrambled to locate her mom's spirit. This thing behind her, this malevolent force had nothing to do with Mom's tragedy. Did it?

The wood railing digging into her ribs creaked. The noise pierced the fog of her self-induced trance. She shook her head, choking and gasping for breath as if she'd just hauled herself out of deep water. She pushed toward the surface of her consciousness, infusing her limp body with strength.

As she gained control of her muscles, she twisted around to confront the force behind her. As she turned, the balustrade cracked beneath her weight.

She teetered on the edge of the landing, her arms flailing at her sides like a pair of useless wings. As she pitched forward, she made a last desperate grab for the railing. Her palm slapped against one of the decorative slats of wood that comprised the balustrade and she clutched it, her fingers wrapping around the wood.

Her body fell and then yanked to a stop. She dangled over the tiled hallway, her body swaying slightly as her arm twisted. She tilted her head back to stare up at the empty landing.

What did she expect to see, a grinning ghost?

A flesh-and-blood person? Something or someone had forced her against that railing so hard it broke. She would've cracked her skull on the tile floor if she hadn't come out of her trance and made a last grab for the slab of wood she now clutched like a lifeline.

Glancing down, she bicycled her legs, trying to judge the distance to the floor or at least the next landing. Could she swing in and make it to the second floor?

She licked her lips. She might get her feet to the next landing, but then what? If she let go and tried to jump, she'd hurtle to the tile.

With her sweaty palms, she tightened her grip on the slab of wood. She swung her legs toward the second-floor landing to test the distance. The toes of her sandals skimmed the balustrade. Maybe… she gasped. During the Tarzan stunt, her piece of railing shifted. If that came loose, she'd be toast.

She gulped back a sob. If she'd stashed her cell phone in the front pocket of her jeans, she could make a call to the Coral Cove P.D., but she'd tucked her phone in the side compartment of her purse.

Was this why Mom had called her to Columbella House, to meet the same fate? Not quite the same. Mom had engineered her own drop from the landing.

Or had she?

The presence behind Kylie had been evil. If she'd channeled Mom's spirit, maybe that same presence had been with her mother up there, too.

Her shoulder ached and her fingers were cramping. How much longer could she hold on?

Her gaze shifted down again and she caught her breath. A glow of light had appeared on the second-floor landing. Maybe she'd been in such a deep trance, she only thought the presence behind her had come from the spirit world. Maybe a human had stood behind her—a human who had come back to protect the secrets of Columbella.

Her heart pounded and her hand slipped a little more. Then she saw it—a grotesquely huge shadow on the second-floor landing, its arms reaching out for her dangling legs.

Chapter Two

The scream ripped through the house and tore into Matt's chest, just like the scream from that drug bust in the club.

Focus, Conner. You're hundreds of miles away from that club and someone else needs you right now.

He turned his flashlight to the denim-clad legs pumping for purchase against thin air.

"It's okay. I'm going to help you. Stop struggling."

A woman sobbed. "Oh, my God. Please, hurry. I'm slipping."

He pressed against the balustrade, leaned over and cranked his head to the side. The woman was holding on to a piece of broken railing from the third-floor landing, her body suspended over nothing but a long drop to the hard tile floor.

Judging by the scream, she didn't have time for him to search for a phone or a ladder. He had to act now. He was good at that—acting first, thinking later.

"Can you swing your legs toward me?"

"Y-yes, but what are you going to do, grab my feet? That's not going to help. You'll probably be left holding a pair of sandals."

Was she trying to tell him how to execute the rescue? Matt straightened his six-foot-four-inch frame. "You get your legs as close as you can, and I'll grab you around the thighs. I have a good view of your hips from here. I'll yank you toward me, and even if you don't clear the railing I can hold on to you."

"I don't know."

Matt blew out a breath. Did she want to be rescued or crack her head open on some old tiles?

"Do you want me to call the Coral Cove Fire Department? I left my cell in my hotel room. Or I can go to the basement and find a ladder."

"No! I can't hold on much longer."

"That's what I thought. Start swinging."

The legs in the skinny jeans swayed like reeds in the wind. The woman grunted and the legs began to swing back and forth.

Matt bellied up to the balustrade, stretching out both arms. "On the count of three, let go and propel yourself forward."

The voice came back, strong and sure. "Okay."

"One…two…three."

The legs hurtled toward him and he cinched his arms around her thighs. As she let go of the railing above, her body jerked but he yanked her toward his chest, stumbling backward. Something smacked the railing. He hugged the body tighter and threw himself back against the wall.

He crashed into the plaster and fell sideways, all the while clutching the soft body to his solid frame. His back hit the floor and still he clung to the woman, taking her down with him.

The back of his head thumped against the hard wood floor. He sucked in a breath, a heady perfume flooding his nostrils, and realized his nose was buried between a pair of luscious breasts in a soft cotton T-shirt.

The woman on top of him gurgled once, scooped in a deep breath and rolled from his body. They lay on their backs, side by side, chests rising and falling.

Matt sat up, wincing as his ribs expanded. He flexed his fingers and glanced at the woman panting next to him, a swath of dark hair across her face. "You okay?"

She nodded. "Thanks."

His gaze traveled the length of her body. Her black T-shirt molded to her upper torso, revealing a sliver of skin above the waistband of her tight jeans. Blue polished toenails peaked from a pair of glittery sandals. And that hair.

A sense of familiarity jolted him. Long, black hair whipping through the elevator doors, a flash of green eyes. He bent over the prone form and brushed the hair from her face.

Sculpted black brows snapped to attention over a long, narrow nose. Nostrils flared.

"You!"

Kylie Grant struggled to a sitting position, nearly clipping his chin with her head. He jerked back, his jaw hardening.

"So you do recognize me. At the hotel, you acted like you'd never seen me before in your life."

Her cat eyes narrowed. "Who says I recognize you from anywhere other than the hotel?"

"Cut it out, Kylie. We were in the same class at Coral Cove High."

"Same class, different universe."

"You and your goth friends occupied a universe all to yourselves." Dread pumped through his veins, and he pointed a finger at the ceiling. "Were you trying to off yourself up there and then changed your mind?"

Her jaw dropped and she scooted away from him. "Absolutely not. I was…I was…"

Matt smacked his forehead. Leave it to Mr. Sensitivity to stick his size-thirteen shoe in his mouth. Kylie's mom had committed suicide in this very house. "I'm sorry."

She huffed out a breath and scooted farther

away, pinning her back to the wall. "Just because you probably saved my life, it doesn't give you license to act like a jerk—although you never needed a license before."

He let that zinger zap him right between the eyes. He deserved it. "What *were* you doing up there? Did the railing break away?"

"Yeah." She hunched her shoulders, her gaze darting to the ceiling. "I was leaning over the railing and it snapped. Luckily, I was able to grab on to a stationary piece of wood, or at least mostly stationary."

He rose to his haunches and gripped the railing. "A lot of wood in this place is worm-eaten. I didn't know the house was this bad. Where's Mia St. Regis?"

"I have no clue, probably running a major fashion house." She drew her knees up to her chest and wrapped her arms around her legs. "What are *you* doing here?"

He raised his brows at her accusatory tone. "Uh, it's a good thing I was here…to save you."

Her eyes, resembling a pair of emeralds, glittered in the flashlight's beam. Kylie had always seemed remote and untouchable in high school. Not that he'd wanted to touch her…then. She'd hung out with a weirdo artsy crowd, and he was enough of an outcast himself that he didn't need to court any of his own kind.

He stood up, stretching to his full height. "I was exploring."

Kylie Grant didn't need to know his business in town. Once he started his investigation, his purpose in Coral Cove would come out soon enough. But by that time, maybe Kylie would be on her way. Her presence at the hotel meant she didn't live in town…unless she was visiting someone at the hotel.

She scrambled to her feet, her shiny sandals catching the light and winking in the gloom. Leave it to Kylie Grant to treat a visit to a haunted house like it was some kind of prom.

"Looks like exploring this house can be hazardous to your health." She flicked her long black hair behind her shoulders and it rippled down her back.

She glided past him and he caught a whiff of her musky perfume. She'd left the same scent in the hotel elevator and he'd gotten a strong dose of it when he'd planted his face between her breasts.

"I'm going upstairs to get my purse and flashlight."

He swung the flashlight forward, waving it back and forth. "You're going to need this to make your way up there."

She held out her hand, and he rested the flashlight against his chest. "I'll come with you."

He clumped up the stairs behind her, his motorcycle boots thumping against each step. How had she not heard him from the third floor? When she crashed through the balustrade, she didn't even call out for help. Matt hadn't been sure what had caused the ruckus until he saw her dangling in midair. He hadn't realized anyone else was in the house.

As he followed her up the stairs, he aimed his flashlight right at her sexy behind encased in those tight jeans. Who knew Kylie Grant had a derriere like that? All through high school she'd worn long, black skirts and silver-studded boots, which probably made her look chubbier than she really was.

Kylie spun around when she reached the third-floor landing, and Matt shifted the light to her face.

Her lips formed a thin line as she wedged a hand on her hip. How did she know he'd been checking out her assets?

"Maybe you'd better go first." She tilted her chin toward the dark landing. "You know, rotten wood and all."

He skimmed the light along the floor. "Didn't you say you had a flashlight?"

"Must've burned out. I left it on the floor next to my purse."

He squeezed past her on the top step and inhaled her perfume again—made him think of dark, mysterious ladies.

She stiffened.

Maybe those stories about Kylie being a mind reader were all true. Matt took two steps toward the broken banister and hunched his shoulders. "It's cold up here."

Kylie drew up beside him and nodded. Then she dipped and scooped up her purse and flashlight. She flicked the switch and another beam of light zigzagged across the jagged wood of the balustrade.

"It does work." Matt didn't recall seeing any light from the third floor as he'd made his way up to the second earlier tonight. He hadn't seen or heard a thing until that crash.

"So, what do you think?" Kylie nudged a piece of wood hanging on by a few splinters. "Rotten?"

He broke off the piece and examined it beneath the light. "It doesn't look that bad, but you never know with old houses."

"You never know."

Matt didn't know if it was the damp chill seeping into his bones or the almost feral look in the lady's eyes, but he wanted out of here.

He placed a hand on Kylie's arm to draw her back from the abyss. "I didn't even ask if you were okay. How's your shoulder?"

She rotated it. "Fine, a little sore."

"Bet you could use a drink. I know I could." Actually, he could use a few, but he never overindulged...ever. At least not with alcohol. But other pleasures? Kylie's skin felt smooth and warm to his touch, and she hadn't even jerked away from him. Maybe saving her life had given him some stature in her eyes. God knows, he hadn't had any before. She'd whipped right past him in the elevator, barely turning when she'd muttered her apology for bumping his shoulder.

"A—a drink?" She'd pivoted on her toes to face him and with her eyes wide, she looked ready for flight.

"Yeah, you know, that wet stuff we pour down our throats?"

Her long lashes dropped over her eyes and she finally shook him off. "I wouldn't have guessed drinking was high on your list of fun activities, given your background."

A slow smile curved his lips. She remembered more about him than she let on, but if she thought that shot was enough to deter his sudden fascination with her, she was as loony as her mom was reported to be.

"One drink. Our hotel even has a bar in the lobby. So we can have a drink and go to bed."

Her lashes flew open.

He kept the smile on his face and shoved one hand in the pocket of his jeans. "You in your bed. Me in mine."

She glanced up at the railing where both her and

her mother's bodies had dangled and shrugged. "I could use a drink."

Matt followed the taillights of Kylie's car back to the Coast Highway and then through the downtown streets of Coral Cove. He was probably way out of line renewing his acquaintance with Kylie. He had a job to do and couldn't afford the distraction.

His hands tightened on the handlebar of his Harley. The last time he'd mixed pleasure with work, it had ended badly. But he had no intention of even telling Kylie about his business in Coral Cove. For all he knew, she'd be on her way out of town tomorrow.

He could enjoy a drink with a pretty girl, couldn't he? He didn't have to tell her his life story. Or listen to hers. Or bed her. Not that he'd get that lucky with Kylie.

He didn't know why she'd agreed to a drink since half the time at Columbella she looked like she wanted to do him bodily harm. Must've been shaken by that fall. And who could blame her? If she hadn't cracked her skull on that floor, she would've at least broken a leg or two.

Fate brought him to Columbella tonight. She must've been on her way here when he ran into her on the elevator. He'd practically followed her over. Maybe things were looking up. About damned time.

While she pulled into the guest parking lot, Matt parked his motorcycle in front of the hotel and kicked down the stand. He pulled off his helmet and tucked it under his arm as she strolled toward him.

She leveled a finger at his bike. "Still riding motorcycles."

"For disliking me in high school, you sure do remember a lot about me."

"You were kind of hard to miss. I think you reached your full height in ninth grade, didn't you?"

He opened the hotel door for her. "Nah, I was probably about six two in ninth grade—still had a few inches to go. You were hardly inconspicuous yourself."

"Me?" She smiled for the first time that night, a slow, sultry lift of one side of her mouth. "I always thought I flew under the radar."

Kylie weaved through the tables in the hotel lobby bar and made a beeline for the grinning bartender. Matt would've preferred one of those little tables with the nuts in a plastic cup, but Kylie settled on a bar stool and planted her elbows on the shiny mahogany.

"I'll have a glass of chardonnay, anything from California, and he'll have…" She raised one eyebrow in his direction without much interest.

"I'd like a beer. What do you have on tap?"

"We have a good microbrew from Avila Beach."

"Sounds good."

Matt perched on the edge of the bar stool next to Kylie's. "Do you want to sit at a table?"

"I'm good here."

She'd been the one hanging from a banister, so he let it go. But he didn't plan on letting her off easy. "What brings you back to Coral Cove and what were you doing at Columbella House?"

She smiled her thanks at the bartender and took a sip of the light gold liquid from her glass. She considered Matt over the rim of that glass. "Isn't it obvious what I was doing at Columbella?"

Matt took a swig of beer and wrapped his hands around the mug. Was this a trick question? Any ideas he'd had about this encounter being an easy, sexy flirtation just fell flat. Kylie didn't do easy… but she had the sexy part down to a T.

"Uh, were you exploring like me?"

She snorted into her wine and he found it oddly appealing. "Come on, Matt. You know my mom killed herself in that house, hung herself from that very landing."

"So were you paying your respects? Putting old demons to rest?"

"Old demons." Her nostrils flared and she flung back her long, black hair looking…witchy.

Like a totally hot, sexy witch.

"I guess you could say that." She tossed back

half the wine and turned toward him, her knees bumping his thigh. "You know I'm a psychic, don't you?"

He choked on his beer, and it came fizzing out his nose. He grabbed a cocktail napkin and hid behind it. Had he known that? The kids in high school used to say Kylie could read minds or tell fortunes, but he just figured they'd said that because Kylie's mom was some kind of gypsy fortune-teller. He just thought the mom was nuts. That's what Matt's dad used to say anyway—not that you could ever trust anything that came out of the old man's mouth.

"You didn't know?" Kylie hunched forward, her hands on her knees, the tips of her long hair brushing his thighs.

To hell with the fortune-telling. He wanted to kiss her right now.

She backed off and took another sip of her wine. Must've read his thoughts on that one, but it wouldn't take much of a psychic to figure out his intentions since the crotch of his jeans had suddenly tightened and he was pretty sure he'd been staring at her luscious pink lips.

He cleared his throat. "I guess I knew that, sort of. So that's why you're back in Coral Cove?" He waved his arm toward the lobby. "Because if you're staying here, I figure you're just visiting."

"It's not exactly a visit, not social anyway." She

ran a fingertip along the rim of her glass. "And the stuff with my mom…it's not my primary purpose for being here."

He waiting politely, taking another sip of his beer, but she didn't finish her thought, and he was left wondering about her primary purpose for being in Coral Cove. Instead, she wiggled her fingers in the air, signaling the bartender. "We'll close out now, unless…" She threw a glance his way.

"No, I'm good, and I'll get this."

"That's not necessary. In fact, I owe you."

As she reached for her purse, her cell phone rang. She checked the display and said, "Excuse me a minute. I have to take this."

She swiveled away from him and hunched over the bar.

Boyfriend? Husband? He hadn't even asked. Didn't want to know.

He lifted his hip from the bar stool to retrieve the card to his room and leaned toward Kylie, not that he was trying to eavesdrop or anything.

Her low, musical voice reached his ears. "Nothing yet, Mrs. Harris. I'll call you as soon as I have something."

A muscle ticked in Matt's jaw. Mrs. Harris?

Kylie clicked her phone off and dropped it back into her purse. "Sorry. I was supposed to call that person earlier and got completely sidetracked."

"By your mother."

"Uh-huh." She made a grab for the check. "I really didn't take that call to avoid paying the bill."

He scribbled his signature and room number on the bill and shoved it toward the bartender. Harris, common name. There were lots of Harrises in the world, right?

The man on the bar stool next to Kylie's spun around, a fake smile claiming half his face.

"Kylie Grant, right?"

Kylie jerked back from the man's eager-puppy-dog enthusiasm. "That's right. Oh, you're Tyler Davis."

"Correct." The man's teeth gleamed in the low light of the bar. "Mayor Davis now."

"Mayor of Coral Cove? That's—" she turned to Matt and rolled her eyes "—impressive."

"I heard a rumor about your presence in town, Kylie. Is it true?"

"Depends on the rumor." She narrowed her eyes and Matt almost felt sorry for Mayor Davis as a chill settled on the bar.

"Not a good idea, Kylie." Davis wagged his finger in Kylie's face and Matt felt like breaking it off. "We should let sleeping dogs lie."

"And murdered dogs? Should we let those lie, as well, Mr. Mayor?"

Matt drew his brows over his nose and tried to catch Kylie's eye, but she'd zeroed in on Davis.

"The girl ran off. There was never any evidence of foul play, and with the Coral Cove Music Festival about to get underway we don't want any bad publicity surrounding the event."

Matt froze and his jaw tightened. What the hell was Davis talking about?

Kylie's lip curled. "You were mayor at the time Bree Harris disappeared, too, weren't you? You and that Chief Evans. That's why there was no evidence of foul play—you and the chief weren't looking for any."

Davis hopped off the stool. "Just don't stir up any trouble for the festival. This town has endured enough this summer. We deserve to end it on a high note."

Kylie muttered something under her breath as Davis sauntered away, stopping to shake hands with a couple by the window.

Matt planted his hands on his knees and swiveled around to face her. "What are you doing in Coral Cove, Kylie?"

She blew a wisp of hair from her face. "I guess you can't keep secrets in small towns, or at least not many. I'm here to investigate the disappearance of Bree Harris. She fell off the face of the earth at the time of the music festival three years ago."

Matt squeezed his eyes shut and pinched the bridge of his nose. This wasn't happening.

She touched his forearm and he nearly jumped out of his skin. It was the first time she'd voluntarily touched him all night…and it felt good. At least it would've if she were here for a different reason.

"What's wrong with you? Ever since that joke of a mayor stopped by, you've looked like a volcano ready to blow its top."

He skimmed his fingers through his hair. "You're in Coral Cove to do a job, and that job is finding Bree Harris. Did her parents hire you?"

She tilted her head and her long hair slid over one shoulder. "Well, sort of. Her mother hired me. Why? What's wrong?"

Matt smacked the bar and shoved to his feet. "What's wrong? Bree Harris's father hired me to do the same job."

Chapter Three

Kylie dropped back onto the leather stool from which she'd half risen. Matt Conner was here for Bree Harris? She pressed the heel of her hand against her forehead.

Matt Conner. What had she heard about the bad boy of Coral Cove High through the grapevine over the years? She'd been so preoccupied by her mission and so disoriented from her fall and so distracted by the way Matt's jeans hugged his...

She shook her head. She'd never bothered to ask him what he did for a living.

Cop. That's what she'd heard. LAPD. The ludicrousness of Matt becoming a cop had even filtered into her universe.

She grabbed her drained wineglass and dumped the final few drops of wine down her throat. What was a cop doing out of his jurisdiction working a three-year-old missing persons case?

He'd been watching her through dark slits of

eyes, his sensuous lips a stern line. At what point during this wild night had she noticed his lips?

"I-in what capacity are you here?" She wasn't going to give him the satisfaction of revealing how much she knew about his life since he'd left high school. She'd already done that and hadn't liked the smug look on his face.

He crossed his arms over his massive chest, and Kylie swallowed. Hadn't he been tall and skinny as a teenager? Now he was tall and...built.

"I'm a private investigator. Mr. Harris hired me to look into Bree's disappearance." He shifted back, almost straddling the stool. "He didn't tell me I'd have a partner."

A P.I., not a cop. The grapevine was wrong.

She grabbed her purse from the bar and hitched it over her shoulder. "I don't work with partners."

"You call what you do work?"

"Do you even know what I do?"

He snorted. "I have a pretty good idea. You sit in front of a Ouija board and say in a spooky voice—*Where's Bree?*"

The blood pumped hot and fast through her veins and it had nothing to do with the way Matt's T-shirt molded to his perfect pecs. "You're a bigger idiot now than when you were riding fast bikes and playing loud music in high school."

Okay, she had to stop thinking about the love-hate obsession she'd had with Matt when she was a stupid teenager.

She drew in a deep breath and tucked her hair behind one ear. "I've worked with police departments all over the country, even the FBI, to help with cases. And my success rate is phenomenal. How many cases have you solved lately? Or have you been too busy following cheating spouses around?"

His eye twitched, and his hands curled into fists against big biceps. If she were a man, she'd be very afraid right now.

"I've solved a few cases."

"Yeah, whatever." A thought slammed against her brain and she drew back her shoulders. "You were following me, weren't you? Mayor Whatsisname knew why I was here, so it's no leap that you knew, too. You followed me to Columbella House because you thought I was tracking a lead on the Harris case and you wanted to horn in on it."

"That's ridiculous." He slammed a fist on the bar and the bartender dropped a glass in the sink.

"Really?" Her heart skittered in her chest. "Because it sure felt like someone pushed me through that railing...and you're big enough to do it."

He threw his head back and laughed. This time the bartender and the couple by the window openly stared at them.

"You're nuts. First of all, why would I be pushing you if I was trying to steal your info? Secondly, wouldn't you have noticed someone behind you on the landing? I mean, I'm no ballerina. I think you would've heard me coming."

"I—I…" She bit her lip. Oh, to hell with it, he had her pegged as a loon anyway. "I was in a trance."

That wiped the sarcastic smile right off his ruggedly handsome face.

"You mean like—" he closed his eyes and held his arms out to his sides and hummed "—om."

She poked him in the chest, and his eyes flew open. "A trance, not meditation."

"So what happens in a trance and how do you get there?" He parked his very fine rear end on the bar stool and hunched forward.

She studied him through narrowed eyes. The man could change moods faster than a rat slipping beneath a door. "Are you serious? You really want to know?"

The bartender edged toward them, a towel bunched in his hands. "Are you folks going to order another round?"

"I'll have a club soda, lots of lime." Matt cocked an eyebrow at her. "Do you want another?"

She just might need another glass of wine to unwind from the roller coaster named Big Matt. "Yes."

"Does that prove it?" Matt pointed at the bartender spritzing club soda into a glass.

"What?"

"That I'm serious. I really want to know how you do what you do."

"Even though you don't believe in it."

"You believe in it."

She rubbed the back of her neck and glanced at her watch. "We're going to close this place down."

"It'll be the first time I've closed down a bar, but I'm always up for new experiences." He flicked the straw out of his glass and downed half the fizzy, clear liquid.

Matt's dad had been the town drunk, and Matt obviously didn't want to follow the same path. That gave them even more in common since she had no intention of following Mom's path either.

She peeled her gaze away from Matt's strong hand wrapped around his sweating glass. The man oozed masculinity and confidence. No wonder he'd been annoyed when he discovered she was on the same case. Why hadn't Mrs. Harris told her Mr. Harris had hired a P.I.?

"Trance?"

His low voice, almost an intimate whisper, was enough to put her under again. He *had* entranced her during high school. He was the rebel without a cause, who had all the teenage girls swooning.

And Kylie hated him because even though he

was as much of an outcast as she was, he still went after the popular girls…and got them, much to their parents' dismay. The parental units didn't have to worry for long though, because Matt never had a girlfriend. He swooped in, swept some cheerleader off her feet for a few weeks, shook her pom-poms and then deposited her back onto the football field. Kylie had always figured he'd done it just to piss off the jocks.

She huffed out a breath and took a sip of wine. "Trance."

"How does it happen?"

"It can happen at any time, but I've learned to control it, to block the sensations. Some days I'm in a heightened state of sensitivity."

"Like today."

She nodded. "On days like that, I go with the flow. I don't try to block anything. If I have something from the victim, I can pick up vibes from it. I guess it is sort of like meditation."

He snapped his fingers. "See? I did have it right."

"I close my eyes. I concentrate. Tonight at Columbella…" She hunched her shoulders and gulped another mouthful of wine.

"Rough, huh?" He skimmed his cool fingertips along her forearm. "That house is enough to raise the hackles of someone who isn't even sensitive…like me."

She stared into Matt's dark eyes and got a little lost. At this moment, with his fingers lightly resting on her wrist, Kylie couldn't completely dismiss his sensitivity.

"So you were in one of those optimal states and hightailed it to Columbella—to do what?"

"I already told you, Matt. My mom hung herself from that landing. I went there to…get some closure."

"And instead you fell through the railing." He tapped her wrist bone once before withdrawing his hand. "That's some kinda closure."

"I sensed fear when I was up there." She traced her finger around the base of her wineglass. "I wasn't expecting that."

"Anyone who commits suicide has to experience some fear, or are you implying your mother didn't kill herself?"

Was she? That thought had been a niggling doubt in her mind for a while. "I don't know. The fall didn't give me a chance to sense much more than a swirl of emotions."

"And to sense someone behind you before the fall."

She raised her brows. "Oh, you believe me now? I thought you figured that was a bunch of bull."

"I thought your suspicions of me were a bunch of bull. The rest? You're the medium."

"You're good."

"Excuse me?" He choked on his drink and grabbed a cocktail napkin to wipe his mouth. "I'm good at a lot of things. Which talent are you referring to?"

Her cheeks grew warm in the dim light. Why did everything Matt said have a sexual connotation to it? Or was that her spin?

"When I first told you Mrs. Harris hired me to find out what happened to her daughter, you weren't too happy about it, implied I was a fraud. Now you're cozying up to me and opening your mind to my gift."

His slow smile twisted his mouth, and he waved his hand in the space between them. "This ain't cozy."

"You know what I mean." She crumpled a napkin in her clammy hand. Matt had sex appeal coming out of his pores, but she didn't plan on becoming one more conquest for him. "Why are you so interested in my psychic powers now when fifteen minutes ago you were scoffing at them?"

He hunched a broad shoulder and drained his glass. "I'm a realist. Mr. Harris hired me and Mrs. Harris hired you. Even though I'm not too keen on having a partner, my goal is to give peace to the Harris family, to find out what happened to Bree, get the girl some justice."

Slapped *her* down. Now her infantile comment about not working with partners sounded…infantile.

"Deal." She extended her hand for a shake. His large hand engulfed hers and he applied a quick pressure to her fingers. She extricated her hand from his grasp and drummed her fingers on the bar to keep them busy. "Do you have anything?"

"Just got here yesterday, but I was wondering about the possibility of Brunswick being involved."

"The algebra teacher?"

"The serial-killing algebra teacher."

"Yeah, I heard all about those women he murdered just to prove something to Michelle Girard. Creepy. But how would Bree Harris be a part of that?"

"You know Brunswick also murdered two prostitutes, don't you? A guy like that doesn't decide one day to start killing to impress a woman."

"Have the cops or the FBI looked into a connection between Brunswick and Bree's disappearance?"

"Not that I know of." He tipped his chin at the bartender. "I stopped by Coral Cove P.D. yesterday to request access to the Brunswick files and the Harris report. The chief is a piece of work."

"I haven't heard good things about him since

I've been here. Chief Reese's son, Dylan, is supposed to come back for the job."

Matt grinned as he slid the check in front of him. "I had a very close relationship with Chief Reese."

"How many times did he pull you over on your bike or ticket you for playing your music too loudly or pick you up for being out after curfew?"

"Too many times to count."

"Yeah, I knew that rumor about your being a cop couldn't be true."

Matt's hand, holding the pen, froze over the check. Then he signed it. "Where'd you hear that bit of nonsense?"

She scooted her stool back and hopped off. "I don't know. Through the grapevine."

Matt rapped his knuckles against the mahogany and called to the bartender. "Thanks, man."

Matt maneuvered her through the bar tables with his hand on the small of her back. He left it there when they hit the lobby. And she let him leave it there.

He dropped it all too soon to stab the elevator button. When the doors whisked open on the empty car, he asked, "What floor?"

"Third."

He pressed the number three button and leaned against the elevator car, hands behind his back, a grin claiming his face. "Guess the hotel put everyone working for the Harrises on the same floor."

Kylie's belly flip-flopped. Not only did she get to work with this hunka, hunka burning manhood, she'd be living a few doors down from him. "Coincidence."

"You disappoint me, psychic lady." He reached forward and touched the tip of his finger to her cheekbone. "I thought you'd call it fate."

She held her breath as the rough pad of his finger brushed her skin. If he was trying to seduce her just like he'd done with all those silly girls in high school, he hadn't lost his touch. Not one bit.

He held up his finger. "You had a black speck on your face."

She wiped her hand across the spot, still tingling from his caress…touch…poke. "Probably a flake of mascara. It's been a long day."

The elevator jostled and then settled on the third floor. As he pinned the door open and gestured her through, he said, "Do you want to meet for breakfast tomorrow morning and go over a game plan?"

"You're serious about working together?"

"Deadly."

"All right." Her steps slowed as she reached her hotel room. "I'm in three-twenty-six."

"How about that?" He slid his card key out of his back pocket and flicked it. "I'm in three-thirty-six. Fate strikes again."

She slid her key home and turned her head toward him, her shoulder wedging against the door. "See you tomorrow in the hotel restaurant at nine?"

"Sounds good."

"Thanks again for rescuing me at Columbella. What brought you there anyway?"

"Research." He called over his shoulder as he ambled five doors down.

Kylie slipped into the darkened hotel room and pressed her back against the door. What was she doing? Mrs. Harris had sent her to Coral Cove to do a job, and she'd planned to combine that job with a little investigation of her own into Mom's suicide.

Now here comes Mr. Sex-on-a-Stick and all she can think about is what he's packing in those tight jeans.

She groaned and pushed off the door, flicking on the light. She blinked. Her gaze darted from her gaping suitcase in the corner to her clothes strewn across the room.

With her heart pounding, she tiptoed into the room and poked her head around the bathroom door. She sagged against the doorjamb like she'd been punched in the gut.

Written on the bathroom mirror in her own red lipstick were the words: *Your Next Bitch.*

Chapter Four

As Matt dropped onto the hotel bed and crossed one leg over his knee to pull off his motorcycle boot, someone pounded on his door. He reached for his Glock tucked into the gun bag around his waist, his muscles tensing.

"Matt? Are you in there?"

He zipped up the bag and smiled. Had Kylie picked up on his hints and decided to join forces in more ways than one?

Thump. Thump.

"Matt! I need your help."

That didn't sound like a prelude to a seduction. He launched from the bed and yanked open the hotel door.

"Oh, thank God. You're still here?"

Still here? Where would he go?

He took in her pale face and wide eyes, and his pulse ticked up a few notches. "What's wrong?"

"Come on. My room." She grabbed his arm and tugged.

Any other time, he'd be looking forward to a woman dragging him to her hotel room, especially this woman, but Kylie needed his help, not his...

"Hang on." Pulling away from her, he retreated into the room a few steps. He swept his key card from the credenza and shoved it into his back pocket.

"What's going on?" He followed her down the hall and waited while she tried to shove her card into the slot three times with shaking hands.

He covered her hand with his and plucked the card from her stiff fingers. He inserted it in the door and blocked her entrance. "What am I looking for?"

"It's on the bathroom mirror. A warning."

He unzipped his gun bag again and squared his shoulders as he walked into her room. The warmth of Kylie's body pressed against his back, and if he turned suddenly she'd land right in his arms. Not that he wanted fear to drive her there.

She'd left the bathroom light on, and he charged into the small space. He read the words on the mirror with a tight jaw.

"Wh-what do you think?"

He braced his hands on the vanity and hunched forward. The sweet, cosmetic smell of the lipstick tickled his nose. Must've happened recently for the smell of the lipstick to be lingering.

"I think this idiot couldn't have been in Mrs. Wilson's English class if he uses *your* for *you are*."

A soft sigh escaped Kylie's lips and her upright posture slumped a little. "You don't think it's serious?"

Matt didn't like the idea of some jerk sneaking into Kylie's room and scrawling juvenile messages on her bathroom mirror, but it didn't seem too serious. Not yet.

"Someone was able to get into your hotel room, so don't take that lightly." He smudged the lipstick with the tip of his finger. "Is this your lipstick? And if so, where's the tube?"

"That's definitely my lipstick." She sidled up next to him in front of the mirror, bumping him with her hip, and grabbed a small leopard-print bag from the glass shelf above the toilet. She unzipped the bag and pawed through the contents. "And someone stole it after they used it for a marker."

"The mayor was in the hotel, and he didn't seem too happy about your investigation into Bree's disappearance."

She shook her head and her long hair brushed his arm. "I can't picture Tyler Davis slinking around hotel rooms."

He shrugged. "You never know. You need to report this to the hotel, anyway. Someone broke into your room."

"And stole a lipstick."

"And wrote a threatening, if illiterate, note on your mirror."

Kylie's forehead creased and Matt bit the inside of his cheek. He didn't want to worry her—it probably was that joke of a mayor trying to scare her off.

She gasped and covered her mouth. "He rifled through my bags, too."

She squeezed past him out of the bathroom and he followed her. She pointed to a couple of suitcases on the floor, the contents jumbled. "Anything missing from the bags?"

"I don't know." She crouched down and sifted through her tossed clothing. "It doesn't look like it."

"Maybe just another scare tactic." He snapped his fingers. "Hey, maybe the hotel has a camera on this hallway and we can expose the mayor and throw a wrench into his reelection plans."

The lines stayed in place between her eyebrows, but the corners of her pretty mouth lifted. "That alone would be worth the shock I had when I walked in here."

He met her eyes and lifted his brows. "You mean you didn't sense beforehand that there was a message waiting for you?"

"It doesn't…" She wedged her hands on her hips

and blew out a breath, and then noticed his grin. She punched him in the arm. "Idiot."

He laughed. "Do you want me to go down to hotel security with you to report this?"

"Sure. Maybe I won't seem like a hysterical female then."

He would've expected more hysteria from any woman after knowing someone had been in her hotel room, leaving a creepy message on the mirror and rifling through her bags. He liked Kylie's measured response—not at all what he'd expect from a medium.

Maybe he could partner up with her after all. It might be easier if they didn't have this sexual tension between them because that had screwed things up for him before. But nobody had ever accused him of being a fast learner.

They traipsed down to the empty lobby and reported the break-in to the front desk clerk. He summoned the hotel security guard, who shot down any hopes they had of a camera recording the dirty deed. Then the clerk exchanged Kylie's card key for a new one and promised to ask the hotel maid on duty earlier if she'd noticed anyone suspicious on the third floor. The whole process took less than fifteen minutes.

They paused in front of Kylie's door, and Matt slipped the new card in the slot. The green lights flashed. Pinching the card between two fingers, he held it out to her. "Are you going to be okay?"

She glanced over her shoulder into the room. "Sure."

"I can sleep on…the floor."

She folded her arms, a gesture that had *no* written all over it. "That's okay. I'm good."

His gaze traced the curves of her body, landing on her blue polished toenails peeking out of her glittery sandals. Kylie was a lot more than good. By the time he returned to her face, her lips were pursed into a line of disapproval.

He had to get a grip on this insane attraction he felt for her. He didn't need the distraction, and she wasn't exactly swooning at his motorcycle boots. He coughed and pointed to the door in her room that connected to the room next to hers.

"Do you want me to see if I can move into the next room?" *Protection not seduction.* "It'll save you from running down the hall next time."

Pushing her hair from her face, she quirked an eyebrow. "Next time? Who says there's going to be a next time?"

"I don't think there will be, but just in case."

She lifted her shoulders and he trained his eyes away from the way her rounded breasts strained against the cotton of her T-shirt. "Suit yourself."

"In the meantime—" he smacked the doorjamb "—lock your dead bolt and put the chain on the door. Don't order any room service and don't open the door for anyone…except me."

"Now you sound more like a cop than a P.I. Are we still on for the breakfast meeting tomorrow at nine?"

"We can make it later if you want."

"No. I feel like I've wasted enough time. I need…we need to get back on Bree's case."

"Nine o'clock it is then." Sensing her dismissal, he stepped back into the hallway.

"Good night, and thanks for helping out… again."

"My pleasure, Madam Medium."

Shaking her head, she shut the door on him. He stood with his head cocked until he heard both the dead bolt and the chain. So he sounded more like a cop than a P.I.? He'd have to change that because he'd never be a cop…never again.

THE NEXT MORNING Kylie adjusted the showerhead so the hot water hit between her shoulder blades. Dropping her head, she braced her palms against the tile. That little swing from the third floor of Columbella had done a number on her muscles.

How much worse it would've been if Matt hadn't rescued her.

And what a rescue. Landing on top of his strong, muscled body had almost been worth the ride.

She sighed and cranked off the faucet. If her

adult self could go back and tell her teenage self that Matt Conner was making suggestive comments to her and sleeping down the hall, her teenage self would faint dead away.

Or who knows? Maybe her teenage self would have more sense than to fall for a bad boy in black motorcycle boots. She'd always thought Matt was totally hot, but if he had crooked his little finger her way like he'd done to so many other girls, she probably would've shot him down. Then. Now?

Now she had a job to do—two jobs if she ever hoped to find peace over Mom's suicide. And now that Matt was involved with her other job, she'd have to find a way to work with him while keeping her thoughts above his waist. Unfortunately for her, he had plenty going on upstairs, too.

She stepped out of the shower and rubbed the steam from the mirror with her fist. She'd scrubbed the threatening words from the mirror last night before she went to bed. The hotel security guard wasn't interested in seeing them, and Kylie had no intention of calling the police. She'd been around police departments long enough to know what the cops found serious enough to investigate. Even a small-town department like Coral Cove wouldn't be interested in a few words scrawled on a hotel bathroom mirror.

Would Mayor Davis be petty enough to try to drive her away with lipstick? Probably.

As she put the finishing touches on her makeup, a loud knock on the door made her smear her pink lipstick onto her face. She'd have to try a different brand. This one obviously had a curse on it.

She squinted through the peephole at Matt, wearing cargo shorts and flip-flops today, lounging in front of her door. Annoyingly, her heart lifted at the sight of him.

She yanked open the door. "I thought we were just meeting at the restaurant. I don't need an escort."

His brows shot up. "Wow, wake up on the wrong side of the Ouija board this morning?"

She sealed her lips against the giggle threatening to humiliate her. "That joke's getting a little old."

"Really? Because I could've sworn a saw a smile light those green eyes of yours."

Matt was more perceptive than she gave him credit for. That's what must make him a good P.I. *Was* he a good P.I.? She knew next to nothing about him. Just that standing close to him made her heart race. And touching him made her body flush.

She threw open the door. "Okay, you're mildly amusing. Let me grab my stuff."

She scooped up her purse and swept open the drapes. "It's sunny."

"And it's already warm. Going to be one of those picture-perfect days on the coast."

"You've been already been outside?" She slipped her card key into the side pocket of her purse.

"Went for a run on the beach and took advantage of the hotel gym before the hordes descended."

Her gaze swept up from his solid, flaring thighs to his broad shoulders that tested the fabric of his T-shirt. Of course he'd already hit the gym. A man didn't get a body like that drinking beer in front of the boob tube.

When she finally made it back to his face, he met her gaze with a tilted grin. Oh, yeah, he knew she'd been checking him out. How could she blame him for taking the same inventory of her last night?

They stepped out of the elevator, and Matt nodded toward the front entrance of the hotel. "We don't have to eat here. There are a couple of breakfast places on Main Street."

"Okay. Let's get out of here. The person who broke into my room might still be lurking around the hotel."

Matt held open the door for her and she brushed past him. Even without the motorcycle boots, he towered over her and just about everyone else.

She stopped on the sidewalk and drew in a long breath of salty air.

"Growing up on the coast, that smell gets into

your system, doesn't it? Even down in L.A., I lived as close to the beach as I could get on my salary."

"Lived? You don't live in L.A. anymore?"

His jaw tightened. "I've been traveling for work. How about you? You left Coral Cove for where?"

"I've lived here and there. I'm up in Oregon now, Portland." Truth was, she didn't have roots anywhere. She had no siblings and her father had run out on her and her mom years before Mom's suicide.

"How about the Whole Earth Café?" He pointed across the street at a small café with a blue awning.

"Looks fine to me. Must be new." She stepped off the curb, but Matt grabbed her arm and pulled her back.

"Better not jaywalk here. I heard the chief is always looking for ways to increase the city's revenues."

"Wow, the bad boy of Coral Cove really is a reformed character. No jaywalking?"

They reached the corner and crossed between the yellow lines of the crosswalk. Matt grabbed the door handle of the restaurant and yanked it open, sending the little bell on the door into a tizzy.

Kylie clutched his arm. "Hold on."

She tilted her head to the side to read one of the flyers posted in the window of the restaurant. Tap-

ping the glass, she said, "It's a flyer for the Coral
Cove Music Festival."

"Those have been up for a while. I've been seeing them all over town in the two days I've been
here. Makes sense—it kicks off in a few days."

A shiver of apprehension rolled through her
body as she bent forward to read the small print
at the bottom of the flyer. "Look. A Harlan Sloan
production."

Matt crouched beside her, his breath fogging the
window. "Harlan Sloan was the concert promoter
the year Bree went missing."

"I see you've done your homework."

"Did you figure me for a slouch?"

She shrugged. "Not really. What kinds of cases
do you work mostly?"

"Let's save this conversation for later." He
straightened to his full height and steered her into
the small café.

The hostess waved them to a couple of empty tables on the right side of the room and they snagged
one in the corner—better for plotting and planning…and working. Because this was a working
breakfast, nothing more.

After the waitress took their order, Kylie planted
her elbows on the table. "Okay, so what else do
you have on this case other than the fact that Harlan Sloan was the promoter of the event and tried

to stonewall the investigation into Bree's disappearance?"

"How do you know Sloan tried to stonewall things? From what I could gather, Chief Evans was quick to label this a runaway situation."

"It delayed the investigation because they weren't calling it a missing persons case until a few days after Bree was supposed to be back home getting ready for college."

"According to Mr. Harris and everyone who knew Bree, she wasn't runaway material." Matt took a sip of his grapefruit juice and puckered his lips. "So how did Sloan figure in the picture?"

Kylie dragged her gaze away from Matt's lips and blinked her eyes. "What?"

"Sloan. How was he blocking the investigation?"

"From the reports I read, he wasn't too anxious to give the police information about the roadies on the show or even the performers." Kylie took a gulp of ice water, trying to quench the fire that burned every time she looked into Matt's eyes.

"I guess his attempt to cover up didn't do much good since he wasn't involved in the past two music festivals."

"He's back now."

"So how do you work? You seem to know a lot about the case."

Could she explain her process to Matt? She'd

never gone into details with anyone before. Kylie swallowed her words while the waitress put their plates on the table.

"Can I get you anything else?"

Matt pointed to his egg white omelet stuffed with spinach and mushrooms. "Some salsa, please."

"Coming right up."

She studied his plate with the fruit and dry wheat toast on the side, and then wrinkled her nose at her own cheese and bacon omelet with twin dollops of guacamole and sour cream on the top. "You're too healthy. You make me feel guilty."

"It wasn't just the drinking with my old man." He picked up a slice of toast and added a spoonful of strawberry jam. "He destroyed his health bit by bit until he dropped dead of a heart attack at forty-nine. I'm not going down that road."

"And yet you still ride a motorcycle."

He shrugged and thanked the waitress for the salsa. "What's life without a few risks? But we were talking about you."

"We were?" She crunched into her bacon, getting no enjoyment from its salty goodness as Matt spooned salsa on his healthy omelet.

"I was asking you how you worked because you seem to know a lot of details about the case."

"Oh, yeah. I guess you figured I just closed my

eyes, and all the answers would come to me. On a Ouija board."

"I have to admit, we…I've never worked with a psychic before on a case. Tell me how it's done."

Kylie took a deep breath. "Every case is a little different. I try to find out all the facts first, usually from the police report if I can get it."

"Do you usually get it?"

"It depends. If the police are the ones who hired me, yeah, slam dunk. If the family hired me…" She hunched her shoulders and dabbed her lips with a napkin.

"I can tell you straight-up, Chief Evans is not the most cooperative guy."

Kylie's hand trembled as she stabbed a potato. "Did you see the report?"

"Nope. Not yet."

"Is he going to give you access?"

"If he doesn't, I'll get it anyway." He polished off the last bite of his omelet and eyed her potatoes. "Are you going to eat those?"

"It's good to see you're not perfect." She shoved her plate toward him.

"Me? Perfect? You've got the wrong guy."

Did she? He seemed so right in so many ways.

"We keep getting off topic." He crumpled his napkin and tossed it on the table. "Whether or not you see the police report, what's your next move?"

"I need something in my possession that belonged to the victim."

"What did Mrs. Harris give you?"

Kylie unzipped her bag and pulled out a red scarf with gold thread woven through it. "This was Bree's."

Skimming his hand across the diaphanous fabric, Matt, said, "I take it you can't just hold the thing in your hand and the victim whispers in your ear or something."

"Not exactly." She balled up the scarf and shoved it back into her bag. "I don't see dead people and they don't talk to me. Rather, I sense a situation or I see scenes flash in my head. Sometimes I feel what the victim feels, and sometimes…" She gripped her upper arms and shivered.

"Sometimes what?"

"Sometimes I'm in the killer's head."

Matt tipped his chair back and cocked his head. "You're kidding."

"Unfortunately, I'm not kidding."

"That's gotta be creepy as hell."

"I think that's what…" She trailed off again. Matt didn't want to hear her wild assumptions about Mom. He already thought she was creepy. "Your turn."

Matt squinted at the bill the waitress had just dropped at their table. "Huh?"

"What do you have, and why did Mr. Harris hire

you? Did he find you on the internet? Portland's a long way from L.A."

"It was a referral, and I don't have much on the case. Just what Harris gave me and going through old news stories—Bree was on summer break from the University of Oregon and drove down solo for the concert, hooking up with some locals while she was here."

Kylie nodded. "She hung out in Coral Cove, stayed with the local kids and they attended the first two days of the concert together."

"And then on the third and last day of the concert—" Matt snapped his fingers "—poof, Bree disappeared."

"I never read anything more about those friends, did you?" She snatched the check from his hand. "I'll get this."

"Do you have an expense account?"

"No. Do you?"

"You're on a job, right?"

"Well, yes."

"You're not doing this pro bono, are you?"

"Of course not. Mrs. Harris is paying me."

"But you're paying your own expenses."

"And you're not?"

"It's a business, sweetheart." He plucked the check from her fingers. "And I have an expense account."

"So you're doing this for the money." Just when

she thought Matt had changed. This talk of money and expense accounts left a bitter taste in her mouth.

"Look." He stacked some bills on top of the check and anchored it with a salt shaker. "I want to find out what happened to Bree. I want to give that family some peace and closure. But I also want to get paid."

"Then we need to get our hands on that police report."

"That's the first thing on my list." Matt pushed back from the table. "Do you want to wait here or meet me outside? I have to use the men's room."

"I'll meet you outside because I need to use the ladies' room."

Kylie slipped into the bathroom, cranked on the water and studied herself in the mirror. So Mr. Harris was paying Matt more money than Mrs. Harris was paying her. Why hadn't the couple made a decision together?

She had never talked to Mr. Harris. She'd figured he was handling his grief differently. But since he'd hired Matt to do the same job, maybe Mr. Harris didn't have any faith in psychics.

She'd have to prove him wrong.

Straightening her shoulders, she tossed the paper towel in the trash bin. She poked her head into the crowded dining room of the restaurant where the clink of dishes and silverware set her on edge.

Matt had to be outside already. As she crossed the room, she dodged waiters and waitresses balancing plates in their hands and up their arms. She pushed out the front door and Matt shrugged off the side of the building.

"Ready to tackle that police report?"

"Yep." Kylie took two steps, and the door of the restaurant swung open behind them.

"Excuse me?" Their waitress, her foot propping open the door, was holding out a card or piece of paper. Did Matt stiff her on the tip?

"You left this on the table."

Since Kylie was closer to the waitress, she took what she now saw was a photo, from her hand. "We didn't leave..."

Kylie's mouth went dry as she stared at the picture pinched between her shaky fingers. Matt hovered behind her. "What is it?"

She held up the photo, facing him. "It's a picture—a picture of Bree. Where did it come from?"

Kylie swiveled her head toward the door of the restaurant, but the waitress had already gone back to her other customers.

Matt plucked it from her hand and turned it over. "Just great. This is more than a picture, Kylie."

He shoved the photo beneath her nose and Kylie

gasped at the block letters on the back of the picture. Another day, another message.

She's dead.

Chapter Five

Excitement fizzed through Matt's veins. Someone had made an effort to communicate with them. And that someone might still be in the restaurant.

He yanked open the door. "Let's see what the waitress has to say about this…unless you can put the picture to your forehead and get a reading on who left it at our table."

"It doesn't…" She sighed and pushed past him, back into the crowded dining room, buzzing with conversation and activity.

If he had known it was this much fun to tease Kylie about her special powers, he would've tried it years ago.

"She's over there." Kylie pointed toward the kitchen, where their waitress was leaning against a counter, waiting for an order to come up.

Threading his way through the tables, Matt scanned the room for anyone taking a particular interest in him or Kylie, but everyone seemed more interested in their food and their own companions.

Matt tapped the waitress on the shoulder. "Excuse me. That wasn't our picture. Did you see anyone near our table after we left?"

"Wheat, not sourdough." She shoved the plate back across the chrome counter and planted her hands on her hips. "What's that, sweetheart?"

Kylie shifted beside him, covering her mouth with her hand.

Matt rolled his eyes at Kylie. "The picture. It's not ours. Someone else left it there. Did you see anyone around our table?"

"Just the busboy, Richard." The waitress narrowed her eyes and surveyed the room. She pointed to a tall, gangly teen clearing a table by the window. "There he is. Slow as molasses, too."

Matt placed a hand on the small of Kylie's back and steered her through the tables toward the window. Richard was sweeping imaginary crumbs from the booth, one earbud from his iPod dangling over his shoulder.

Kylie whispered, "I can tell already, he's not going to be any help."

"Is that your psychic powers kicking in?"

Sliding the photo of Bree onto the table in front of Richard, Matt asked, "Did you see who left this picture at the table over in the corner?"

"Huh?" The teen yanked the other earbud out

of his ear and tinny music battled with the noise from the restaurant.

Matt tapped the photo. "This picture, someone left it on our table."

Richard nodded. "With the check. It was under the salt shaker with the check."

"Did you see who put it there?"

"I thought you did."

"You didn't see anyone near our table after we left?"

"I didn't notice." He jerked his thumb at the waitress, taking an order at the same table where they'd just eaten. "Arlene's always getting on my case for being slow, but I thought you guys were coming back so I let the table sit. The picture was there when I cleared the table."

"Okay, thanks." Matt reached into the deep pocket of his cargo shorts and pulled out one of his new cards, wrapped a five-dollar bill around it, and slipped it to Richard.

"Thanks, man." He stuffed the card and the money into the front pocket of his jeans. "I'll let you know if I see anyone else running around leaving pictures."

They shuffled out the front door, and Matt threw a last glance over his shoulder.

"You want to question everyone in there, don't you?"

"That's not a bad idea."

She put a hand on his forearm. "Think about it. If the person who left that picture wants to talk to us but wants to remain anonymous, he or she is not going to be thrilled if we raise a fuss in the restaurant."

"You're right. We want this person to contact us again…unless this is a prank."

"It could be, but it seems like a lot of trouble to go through for a prank. And where would someone get a photo like that of Bree?"

Matt moved into the sun and held the picture close to his face. "It was taken here, at the beach."

Kylie leaned in close to study the picture with him. "That beach could be anywhere."

"Look at the rock formation behind her." He traced his finger along the glossy surface of the picture. "Look familiar?"

"It's the beach below Columbella House."

"Put it in your bag for safekeeping, and let's go find out from that police report who might have taken a picture of Bree while she was here."

Kylie stepped off the curb and Matt caught her hand. "You really need to get out of the habit of jaywalking. Don't tell me you do it in Portland."

She rolled her eyes at him. "This is Coral Cove, not Portland."

"If you're more worried about your bank account than your safety, you'll take a hit there—and you don't even have an expense account. Didn't I just tell you the police chief likes racking up the revenue through fines?"

"I know all about Chief Evans. He was here when my mom died."

"I just hope he has the report he promised me yesterday."

They crossed the street at the crosswalk and Matt pulled open the door of the police station for Kylie. Just like yesterday, the smells of furniture polish and the sounds of the tapping on the keyboard caused the memories to flood back. Some good—like the times Chief Reese hauled him and his buddies in for some harmless, but hilarious prank—and some not so good—like the times Matt had to pick up his old man for being drunk in public.

Kylie nudged him in the ribs. "Stop reliving the glory days."

The cop at the front desk looked up when they stepped up to the counter. "Can I help... Oh, you're the P.I. from yesterday."

"That's me." Matt spread his arms. "Do you have the case report I requested?"

Officer Dickens shifted his gaze to the right and then back to Matt's face. "Yeah, we have it."

"Okay, turn it over." He rapped on the countertop with his knuckles. He didn't much like the cop's demeanor. Either they had the report or they didn't.

The cop swiveled his chair toward an overflowing in-basket and pulled out a manila envelope with a black scrawl on it. He slapped the envelope on the counter in front of Matt. "Here you go."

"That's it?" Kylie echoed his own thoughts as he swept the thin envelope off the counter.

Matt retreated to a plastic chair against the wall and opened the envelope. He shook out the stack of papers and raised his brows at Kylie over the top of the measly stack.

"Not much of a report." She hunched forward and pinched the report between two fingers.

Matt thumbed through the pages and hissed through clenched teeth. "The length is only half the problem. Look at this."

He shuffled through the pages, dotted and scarred with black marker.

Kylie snatched a page from the batch and ran her finger along the lines. "This is useless. All of the important information, such as names of witnesses, has been redacted."

Matt shoved up from his chair and strolled back to the counter, smacking the report against his palm. He tossed it onto the countertop. "This isn't exactly what I had in mind, Officer."

Officer Dickens's gaze shifted again, and then trailed to his computer screen. "That's the report we have."

"All of the vital information has been redacted."

"A lot of reports are like that…sensitive information. You should know that."

Matt's fist landed on the counter. "How am I… how are we supposed to investigate this young woman's disappearance if key information is missing?"

"Is there a problem out here?" Chief Evans strode into the reception area from the back offices.

"Yeah, there's a problem." Matt scooped up the pages and shook them at Evans. "This so-called report is useless. I need the witness names, the possible suspects, the autopsy report."

The chief stuffed his hands in his pockets and lifted his shoulders. "This is an open case. We have to protect the identities of these witnesses."

"That's bull. Social security numbers, sometimes addresses, driver's license numbers—those are typically redacted but not witness names."

Kylie took a step forward and hunched over the counter. "And you're ensuring the case will remain open if you refuse to give us pertinent information."

The chief's gaze flicked toward Kylie and then back to Matt. "Big-city departments may do things differently, Conner, but here in Coral Cove we strive to protect our residents."

Kylie huffed out a breath. "You're doing a bang-up job—serial killers, bank robbers stalking little boys. Coral Cove ain't what it used to be."

Chief Evans narrowed his eyes. "Really? I guess I wasn't here in the good old days when Coral Cove had crazy gypsy ladies telling fortunes and the town drunk passing out on park benches."

Kylie gasped and a muscle ticked in Matt's jaw. He tightened his fist around the sheaf of papers clenched in his hand. He really wanted to punch that smug face swimming before him.

Matt shoved the papers back into the manila envelope and took Kylie's arm. "We don't need his help, Kylie. He's afraid we'll solve what he couldn't, and maybe that big-city police department he's heading out to manage will have second thoughts about hiring him."

He practically had to drag Kylie from the police station. Her fury had her rooted to the floor. When he got her outside, he grabbed her shoulders and turned her to face him. "Take a few deep breaths."

She closed her eyes and although anger still colored her cheeks, her breathing had returned to normal. "That jerk. We're going to have to rely more on my ability to get a reading on Bree than good old-fashioned investigating."

He pinched her chin and her lashes flew open. "Don't worry. The full police report, and a lot more, exists somewhere, and we're going to get all of it."

"Oh, really?" Her chest rose and fell again rapidly, but Matt wanted to believe it was his proximity to her that was causing it this time, not her anger.

"Really."

"And how are we going to do that?"

"We're going to steal it."

KYLIE STUDIED MATT'S FACE, his dark eyes alight with amusement. *He's kidding.*

She laughed. "Not that Chief Evans wouldn't deserve it."

"I'm not kidding. I'm going to steal the report… all of it."

"Matt Conner, you haven't changed a bit."

He held up his hands. "Hey, I never stole anything that didn't belong to me…or should've belonged to me."

"Yeah, like someone else's girlfriend." She covered her big mouth with her hand.

"You can't steal people. They either come willingly…or not." He winked. "Now let's take a look at this report and see what we can glean from it. Maybe it will be enough for you to start your mumbo jumbo stuff."

"If you keep calling it mumbo jumbo, I'm not going to use it to help you. And what about your theft of the Coral Cove P.D.?"

"I have a few ideas. Don't worry. None of them involves you."

"That's good. At least one of us can stay out of jail to work on this case."

He held up the report. "My room, your room or our room?"

"*Our* room?"

"I asked the hotel about moving into the room next to yours. Luckily, it's being vacated today. We can throw open the door between the two rooms and set up a regular command center."

She checked her watch. "It's just after eleven o'clock. I doubt if the room will be ready."

"Your room then."

Matt stopped by the front desk when they hit the lobby and shook his head at her as she waited by the elevator. Guess Matt couldn't get everything he wanted. But she hoped he could get his hands on the complete and unaltered police report.

And her? Did he want her?

He loped toward her with his long stride and easy grin. "You were right. The room next to yours isn't ready yet."

Kylie hit the button for the elevator. "You can't always get what you want."

"Are you referring to that police report, or…"

She bumped his shoulder on her way into the elevator. Just like the first time they'd run into each other. She should've seen that as a premonition. "The police report. I don't know how you plan to steal it."

"Shh." Putting his finger to his lips, he looked both ways. "You don't need to know."

When they got to her room, Kylie hesitated on the threshold. What would she find this time?

Matt nudged her to the side. "Let me take a look first."

She held her breath as he walked into the room, fearless and almost challenging. Great guy to have on your side. If the cops had handed *her* that police report, she probably would've swallowed it and moved onto plan B.

Matt did a sweep of the room and called over his shoulder. "All clear."

Sighing, she let the hotel door slam behind her, and she hung her purse over the back of a chair. "You know what was weird about that message?"

"The fact that it was misspelled?"

"No. The message basically admitted that Bree Harris was dead by threatening that I would be next."

"The message on Bree's picture said the same thing...not that I ever thought otherwise." Matt dropped the file on the table by the window. "Did you?"

"Not really. Her scarf..."

"Did you already try some mumbo...to get a reading on the scarf?"

"Not yet. My supposition about Bree came from common sense. Where would a college girl like that go?"

"True, but she could've died from an accident, not murder."

"Not according to that message on my mirror."

"Maybe someone was with her at the time of the accident, someone who didn't bother to get help or report it."

"Or someone who was too drunk or high to help her."

"Either way—" Matt tapped the manila envelope "—we're here to find out and give some peace to Mr. and Mrs. Harris."

"And to make some money."

"There's always that." He yanked a chair out from the table and patted the seat. "Come over here and let's have a look at this police report together."

"I have some water in my mini fridge. Do you want some?"

"Sure."

Matt waited until she brought two bottles of water to the table and took her seat before he dropped into the chair across from her. He opened the file and shook the contents out onto the table.

Shuffling through the pages, Kylie said, "Pathetic. This isn't like any report I've ever seen when I've worked with P.D.s. I get the whole thing."

"That's because you're working with the cops, not against them, like we apparently are here."

"So you've worked with the LAPD?"

"Huh?" Matt dropped the paper in his hand and jerked his head up.

"Chief Evans mentioned something about how you might be accustomed to the way big-city police departments do things, so I thought you might've worked with the LAPD before."

He ducked his head and thumbed through a few more pages. "The LAPD doesn't work with P.I.'s, but the detectives will cooperate, especially on a cold case where the victims' families have hired outside help."

"I've worked with a lot of departments across the country, but never the LAPD." She craned her neck to peer at the first page of the report, which Matt held in one hand. "Can we move to the love seat, so we can sit next to each other? At this distance, I'm going to get a crick in my neck."

"Good idea." He gathered the papers and moved to the love seat.

Kylie settled on the cushion next to him. "Okay, let's start from the beginning and see what we can glean from this mess."

As she leaned over, the seat cushion dipped and her leg brushed Matt's muscled calf. If she jerked away, it would only prove his nearness affected her. She scooted closer until they were hip to hip.

Bending his knees, he braced his feet on a small table and propped up the report on his legs. "First page, standard missing persons stuff."

Matt read aloud while Kylie followed his finger trailing beneath each line. He started saying *beep* every time he ran into a blacked-out word, mostly names.

She pushed against his solid shoulder. "Okay, will you stop doing that? It's really annoying."

"You're right." He took a swig of water and re-settled the pages on his thighs. "Where were we?"

"The place where Bree tells beep and beep that she's going to make a stop before meeting them for the last day of the concert."

Matt cleared his throat. "The victim met up with...blank and blank at the concert and stated that she'd visited blank on Cressy Road. Aha! They forgot to blot out that one."

Kylie choked on the water going down her throat. "What? Let me see that."

She grabbed the report from Matt's lap and stabbed her finger at the paragraph he'd just read. "Cressy Road."

"That's right. At least it's something."

Kylie's heart hammered so hard, she placed a hand over her chest as if to keep it in place. "Matt, I lived on Cressy Road."

"Did you? Kind of out of the way, isn't it?"

She dropped the report back in his lap and pinned her trembling hands between her knees.

"What's wrong, Kylie?"

"Don't you get it? Bree Harris went to see my mother before she died…before they both died."

Chapter Six

Matt's eyebrows shot up to his hairline. "How did you get all that from one reference to Cressy Road?"

She bounded up from the love seat and paced toward the window. "Have you ever been to Cressy Road?"

"Sure." He waved his arm. "It's out by the edge of town, kind of rural."

"Kind of rural?" She dragged her hands through her hair, a million thoughts tumbling through her brain. "My mom's house was on a dirt road. Three years ago, she was about the only one left there. It had to be her."

"And what would Bree be doing visiting your mom?"

She widened her eyes and tugged at her roots. "What do you think? She went to her for a reading."

Matt's jaw dropped. "Does that mean your mom could've envisioned Bree's murder?"

"No. I don't know." She took another turn around the room. "If Bree had death hanging over her head, my mom would've been able to sense it. But maybe Bree took a different path that day, leading her to her killer, a path she hadn't planned when she saw my mother. Then Mom wouldn't have known."

"Sounds confusing." Matt scratched his chin.

Kylie perched on the arm of the love seat. "Don't you see, Matt? Bree's disappearance and my mom's suicide are linked."

"Whoa, whoa, whoa." He jumped up from the love seat. "Just because Bree went to your mom for a reading that day doesn't mean their two tragedies are linked."

"It's too much of a coincidence. My mom was one of the last people to see Bree alive, and then she killed herself four months later?"

"Do you think your mother was murdered? Is that what you were trying to find out last night?"

"Maybe she knew something about Bree. Maybe someone wanted to shut her up." A chill rushed through Kylie's body and she gripped her arms. "Just like that message on my mirror—*you're next.*"

Matt took two steps toward her and pulled her into his arms. "I'm not saying you're wrong, but don't get ahead of yourself."

She murmured against his chest, not wanting

to leave the comfort of his embrace. "We need to find out who those other witnesses were. Maybe Bree told them what my mother said."

Matt tapped his temple. "I'm working on it. I already have an idea of how I'm going to get my hands on that report."

Matt's cell phone, jammed into the front pocket of his shorts, buzzed against Kylie's leg and she realized she was still pressed against him.

She wriggled out of his one-armed grasp and stumbled backward.

He offered a steadying hand. "Careful."

Then he dug his phone from his pocket. "Hello? Yeah."

Swiveling the phone away from his mouth, he said, "Front desk."

As Matt finished his conversation, Kylie gathered their water bottles and dropped them into the trash. "Is your room ready?"

"Yeah. Are you going to be okay while I move my stuff over?"

"I'll be fine." She fluttered her fingers at the door. "Go do what you need to do. I have to make some phone calls."

"I'll leave the report with you, and I'll work on getting the uncensored version." He brushed a strand of hair from her cheek. "Don't worry. If your mom is involved in this, we'll get to the bottom of it."

She nodded and then stared at the door as he closed it behind him. The uneasy realization that she believed him crept across her brain. In less than twenty-four hours, she had come to believe that Matt Conner could do anything.

MATT WHEELED HIS SUITCASE into his new room… right next to Kylie's.

Had Kylie's mother really spoken to Bree the day the young woman disappeared? Was she connected to this case? That would be too weird, but in Kylie's world, weird was the norm.

Once they got the full police report, they'd have a better idea of what went down. And he had every intention of getting his hands on that police report.

As soon as he'd seen Annie Summerholdt at the police station the day before yesterday and found out she worked in the records department, he knew he'd be using her services. Not that he'd use their brief flirtation in high school to his advantage, but Annie owed him.

She'd had a big lug of a boyfriend on the football team, and the jerk had somehow gotten the idea it was okay to push his girlfriend around. Until Matt had seen him one day shove Annie into a wall.

He took the guy down and Annie had the good sense to break up with him after that. Yeah, she owed him.

Matt took out his cell phone and fell across his

newly made up bed. Annie had punched in her number herself.

"Coral Cove P.D., records."

"Hey, Annie, it's Matt Conner."

"Hi, Matt. Didn't think I'd be hearing from you so soon, or at all."

"I have a favor to ask of you."

"Hold on." Some rustling and clicking came over the line before Annie came back on. "You want the Harris files."

"Wow, you're quick."

"I heard them talking today about how they pulled one over on you by giving you a heavily redacted file. It's not even the full file."

"Yeah, that Chief Evans is a piece of work. What's he afraid of?"

"I don't know. He takes a lot of his marching orders from Mayor Davis. He's very concerned with the town's image, especially before he leaves for his new job. Can't blame him for that."

"If they're so concerned with the town's image, you'd think they'd want an old case solved. So can you help me out?"

"I'd really like to, Matt, but I could lose my job if they discovered that file missing."

"I don't want you to lose your job."

"If there was some other way to get you that file without taking it from the station or making copies of it and slipping it out, I'd do it. You literally saved my life in high school."

"I have a way, Annie, if you're up to it."

"What?"

"I have a small camera that's good for document photography. You can take a picture of every page in the report. No copy machine trail, no fax trail, no walking out with papers. What do you say?"

She blew out a breath. "I can do that."

Matt rolled onto his back, his feet dangling from the foot of the bed. "You're a lifesaver."

"How are you going to get the camera to me?"

"Let's make it an unexpected meeting, just in case."

"I'll be at Burgers and Brews tonight. Can you make it over there around…seven o'clock?"

"I'll catch up with you there."

Matt ended the call and tossed his cell phone up in the air. This P.I. stuff was easier than he thought it would be.

A sharp rap at his door was followed by a voice. "Room service."

Matt had ordered lunch before he moved his stuff over, and had gotten two of everything in case Kylie wanted to join him. He bounded off the bed and pulled open the door to his room.

The waiter, a twentysomething with longish hair and a soul patch, hunched over the cart laden with chrome-domed serving dishes. "Room service, right?"

"You have the right room." Matt held the door open and the cart trundled by with the waiter at the helm.

He hoisted the tray. "Where do you want this?"

"You can put it on the table behind you."

As the waiter placed the tray on the table, the sleeve of his white jacket rose on his arm, displaying a neon green wristband.

Something clicked in Matt's memory. "What's the wristband for?"

"This?" The waiter hooked his finger around the band. "It's for Rockapalooza."

"The Coral Cove Music Festival?" Matt knew a lot of the local kids called the event Rockapalooza.

"Yeah. I heard the promoter was looking for locals to help with the setup, so I applied. I'm going out there tonight."

Matt added a tip to the check and scribbled his signature. "Is the promoter in town yet?"

"He's here. I haven't met him yet, but man I'd like a permanent gig with his operation." He stuffed the check and the pen in his pocket and wheeled the cart toward the door. "Beats this crappy job."

When the waiter left, Matt knocked on the door that connected his room with Kylie's. "You in there?"

The dead bolt clicked and the door swung open. "How's your room?"

"Just like yours. Do you want to have some lunch? Sandwiches, fries, fruit."

She poked her head into his room and wrinkled her nose. "Yours looks bigger."

"It's just an illusion. My room's cleaner. Lunch?"

"That sounds good about now." She followed him into his room and peeked under one of the dish covers. "I called Mrs. Harris and asked if she could call the Coral Cove P.D. about releasing the unredacted file to me."

Matt shook out one of the napkins as his eye twitched. "Did you tell her about me? About us?"

"Us?"

"Working together."

"I didn't mention you." She picked up a plate with a sandwich and some fruit and perched on the edge of the love seat. "I think maybe that's for Mr. Harris to tell her, don't you?"

"I suppose so." Matt grabbed a sandwich from a plate and wedged a shoulder against the sliding door that led to a small balcony. "Harlan Sloan's in town."

Kylie swallowed a bite of cantaloupe. "How do you know that?"

"The room service waiter is working on the setup tonight. He told me."

She dabbed her fingers on the napkin covering

her lap. "I think we need to see Sloan, ask him some questions."

"I agree. The fact that he stepped back from promoting the show until this year is suspicious to me."

"The police questioned him and his security force. Now it's our turn."

"Let's head over to the concert grounds when we finish lunch, and then we have an appointment at Burgers and Brews."

"An appointment? What kind of appointment?"

He dropped the remainder of his sandwich on the plate and brushed his hands together. "We're going to give a C.C.P.D. employee a camera so she can take pictures of the case file on Bree Harris."

Kylie's fork froze halfway to her mouth. "You're kidding."

"I'm not. I have an in at the department."

"How could you have an in at the department? You just got here two days ago, didn't you?" She placed her fork across her plate and folded her hands in her lap.

"She's someone I knew in high school."

Kylie's folded hands turned into twisted fingers. "Is she expecting some kind of reward?

"It's the other way around. Annie Summerholdt is paying a debt to me."

Her green eyes widened. "Annie? Can you tell me about it?"

He grinned. He liked Kylie's up-front attitude—no passive-aggressive pretending everything's okay and secretly stewing with jealousy. Whoa. Not that Kylie would be jealous of some woman owing a debt to him. Would she?

"It was nothing. Do you remember she used to date that knucklehead Dave Kenner?"

"Dave was more than a knucklehead." She folded her arms and shivered. "He was one mean sucker."

"He used to knock Annie around and one day I caught him in the act, so I…uh…made him stop."

"Wow, who knew you were running around saving the girls of Coral Cove from abusive boyfriends?"

He shrugged, feeling his ears burn. "It just gave me an excuse to kick Kenner's ass."

"If you say so." She carried her plate to the tray and stacked it with the others. "I'm going to brush my teeth and change clothes, and then it's time to rock 'n' roll."

An hour later, Kylie was thanking her lucky stars she'd changed clothes as she clung to Matt's waist on the back of his motorcycle. The wind scrambled her hair around the ill-fitting helmet, and she scooted in closer to Matt's back…not that she could get any closer.

He took the next turn on the Coast Highway, and Kylie clamped her knees against his thighs.

Was he driving like this so she'd be forced to wrap herself around his body?

His announcement about Annie had surprised her. She'd been holding her breath for some admission that he'd rocked Annie's world in high school and now she owed him big-time. Instead he'd been the hero of the story...and he didn't seem to wear that label with any ease.

Of course, when he'd been *her* hero, rescuing her from Columbella, he sure seemed to want to take credit for that. Matt was just as complicated now as when they were teenagers.

He took an exit off the highway, and wended the motorcycle into the low hills, the shade from the multiple trees cooling the air. The rustic setting of the concert grounds lurked around the next bend in the road.

Kylie had been to the festival a few times, but it didn't feature her kind of music or ambience— too many unwashed bodies, too much casual sex, too many memories of Mom trying to pick up extra business from the throngs of hippie-dippie young people who flooded the area. Is that how she'd met Bree?

The bike slowed down as Matt took the final turn, and they began their descent into a small city, teeming with people scurrying around the festival grounds, which was shaped like a giant bowl.

Matt turned his head and whistled. "Crowded."

She yelled over the roar of the motorcycle. "How are we going to find Sloan?"

Cutting the engine of the bike, Matt eased it down a dirt road where people had abandoned their cars in a helter-skelter manner. He found a spot beneath a redwood tree and planted his boots on the ground, strewn with fragrant needles.

Kylie slid from the back, her own sneakers plowing into the soft ground cover. She tugged the helmet from her head and clutched it against her body while Matt secured his bike.

"Sloan will most likely be by the stage, or at least the beginnings of the stage." He pointed to a huge raised platform at one end of the bowl where lights, cables and scaffolds crisscrossed the surface.

"Are they going to be working on this all night?"

"They'd better. They don't have much time before Rockapalooza gets underway. Follow me." He tromped through the trees, making a path for her, and she scurried after him.

"Matt." She grabbed his arm to slow him down. "I have Bree's scarf with me. I'm going to try to get a reading on her before we leave."

He stopped suddenly and she plowed into his back. "Are you sure that's a good idea?"

"That's what I'm here for. That's why Mrs. Harris hired me. I'm not here to be your investigative sidekick."

He wedged a finger beneath her chin and tipped her head back. "Is that how I'm making you feel?"

"No, but I want to do the job I was hired to do."

"I get that. I'll be your psychic sidekick if you want."

Kylie stared into Matt's dark eyes, so sensuous but always with that touch of humor or naughtiness. The noises from the concert setup retreated and the fresh smells of the trees and a whiff of salty air inundated her senses. She felt so in tune with Matt, they could be floating on a cloud all by themselves.

The boy she'd alternately crushed on and despised had turned into one helluva man. If he'd set out to be everything his father wasn't, he'd succeeded.

His face broke into a grin, banishing the spell, and Kylie shook her head. "It's something I need to do on my own."

"Let's get this part over with first."

Ducking into the clearing, Matt held back some branches for Kylie and they both stood on the edge of the bowl taking in the activity.

Matt snorted. "It's probably the hardest these kids have ever worked for anything in their lives."

"You have to admit, it's kind of genius the way Sloan handles this event. He gets a bunch of local kids to do most of the work and pays them in food and an early entrance to the concert so they can get the good places up front. He must be saving a bundle."

"Do you think Bree helped with the setup?"

"Yeah. Yeah, I do."

Entwining his fingers through hers, Matt led the way through the press of people, setting up trash cans and erecting pop-up tents on the sidelines for information, lost and found and first aid. As they got closer to the stage, the noise intensified—pounding, drilling, buzzing. Kylie's nose twitched and she sneezed after breathing in wood dust.

One man commanded center stage, his silver hair glinting in the rays of sun that managed to sneak through the heavy foliage. His black turtleneck, tight jeans and pointed black boots marked him as an outsider among the saggy jeans, baggy T-shirts and flip-flops or work boots of the others.

Matt squeezed her hand. "That's our man."

At that moment, Harlan Sloan jerked his head in their direction and his light-colored, piercing eyes skewered Kylie. She drew in a sharp breath.

He knew.

"Are you coming?" Matt tugged her hand, as he moved toward the steps on the side of the stage.

There were enough workers scurrying around and on the stage that nobody halted their progress, taking them for another set of locals. Matt's confidence carried them all the way to the middle of the stage where he planted himself in front of Sloan.

He stuck out his hand. "Harlan Sloan? I'm Matt Conner. Bree Harris's family hired me to look into their daughter's disappearance three years ago."

Sloan's gaze darted from Matt's hand to Kylie's face before he shook hands with Matt. "I'm afraid I don't know what happened to that poor girl, Mr...."

"Conner. Can we ask you a few questions? I'm sorry—" he gestured toward Kylie "—this is Kylie Grant. The family also retained her services."

Kylie didn't offer her hand and Sloan didn't either, a curt nod his only form of acknowledgment.

"You can ask, Mr. Conner, but I won't be of any help. I did promote the concert that year. I met the girl because she volunteered, but I didn't see her much. And I certainly didn't see her the night she disappeared."

"And yet—" Matt scratched the scruff of his beard "—you didn't work on this event for the two years following Bree's disappearance."

Sloan laughed, an unpleasant sound that caused Kylie to clench her jaw. "And you read all kinds of nefarious implications into that, Mr. Conner? I hope that's not what you used to convince the Harris family to reopen the case."

Matt smiled but it didn't reach his eyes or light up his whole face like his grin did. "I didn't have to convince the Harrises of anything, Mr. Sloan.

And this case can't be reopened because it was never closed—Bree Harris is still missing."

"I can't help you."

"And your roadies? Your security? Are you using the same bunch you used three years ago?"

"I haven't a clue." Sloan gestured around the stage. "But you're welcome to ask them. I'm sure a few of the same workers are on board for this Rockapalooza. Now, if you'll excuse me, I have a lot of work to do."

He turned on his heel and strode backstage, shouting orders.

Through narrowed eyes, Matt watched Sloan retreat. "Smooth operator. What about you? Did the cat get your tongue?"

Kylie shivered. "I don't like him."

Matt studied her face. "Did you get some kind of vibe off of him?"

"Yeah, and not a good one."

"Doesn't seem to mind if we question the hired help though, so let's get busy."

"Right." Kylie tipped her head toward a group of young women securing electrical tape along the wires crisscrossing the stage. "I'll start with them."

"And I'll start with the show roadies." Matt shaped his fingers into a gun and fired at her. "Good luck."

Kylie picked her way across the stage, dodging

people and equipment. She crouched beside the girls, giddy with excitement and bubbling with gossip.

"Hey, can I ask you a few questions?"

The girls turned their shining eyes on her.

"Sure."

"What about?"

"Okay."

Kylie sat down, crossing her legs. "Do you get paid for doing this?"

A pretty redhead shook her curls. "Not with money, but we get wristbands that get us early entrance to the concert on opening day."

"And if we're lucky, we get to meet the band members if we're here when they show up for a sound check." The brunette winked at the other girls.

"Forget the guys." The tall, slender African-American woman snapped her fingers. "I'm here for the free food."

The redhead pushed her. "You are so not here for the food."

Kylie smiled, feeling ancient at thirty. "Have you girls ever heard of Bree Harris?"

The African-American girl and the redhead shrugged. "No. Is she a new act?"

"I know who she is." The brunette bit her lip and glanced at the other two. "When my mom heard I was going to help out with Rockapalooza this year, she warned me to be careful."

The redhead snorted. "Your mom's always warning you to be careful."

"Bree Harris disappeared from this concert three years ago." Kylie wrapped her arms around her legs. "I believe she was working, just like you girls."

"Yeah, that's what my mom told me."

"Maybe she ran off with a musician." The redhead tugged one of the African-American girl's long braids. "Just like Myesha's going to do."

"Only if we take some food with us."

Kylie's announcement about Bree hadn't impressed the girls too much. Only the petite brunette seemed shaken out of the giggles.

Kylie pushed to her feet. "You girls be careful out here. If you see or hear anything weird, tell someone about it, and don't go off with any musicians."

They mumbled and snickered and continued crawling along the edge of the stage, laying down electrical tape.

Kylie's gaze wandered to Matt, left hand in the pocket of his jeans, tattoo snaking up his forearm. All he needed was the long hair he used to have in high school, and he'd fit right in with this rock 'n' roll crowd again.

He caught her eye and gave her a thumbs-up.

Did that mean he was having more success than she'd had with those clueless girls?

Creak. Creak.

At the ear-splitting noise above her, Kylie threw her head back. Huge, round klieg lights teetered on the edge of a wobbling platform. Her brain screamed *run,* but her feet were rooted to the stage, like the proverbial deer, her eyes mesmerized by the lights.

As if in slow motion, the spheres toppled from their perch on a path straight toward her.

Chapter Seven

"Kylie!" Adrenaline pumped through Matt's system so fast and furiously, his feet were moving before his brain had given them the command.

What was she waiting for?

Someone screamed.

Matt didn't have the time or the position to tackle her, so he hooked an arm around her waist and took her with him as he charged past the falling lights.

As his arm plowed into her middle, she expelled a puff of air. A metal pole scraped Matt's hand and he staggered toward the edge of the stage, finally crashing into a man-sized speaker.

The klieg lights hit the stage behind him, bounced once and rolled into the first-row seats.

Matt peered over Kylie's head. Thank God the lights had banged into an empty row. Everyone had seen the catastrophe unfold and had scattered out of the way.

Everyone but Kylie.

Her body, pressed against his, began to shake and her knees buckled. Matt scooped her up in his arms and carried her off the stage. He settled her on the soft grass as people on the stage sprang into action.

"What the hell just happened?" One of the workers stomped across the stage and leaned over. "Is she okay? Miss, are you okay?"

Matt ran his hands along Kylie's arms. "You okay?"

She nodded, her eyes wide and glassy.

"She's fine, just shaken up. Anyone have some water, or better yet some booze?"

Asking for booze at a concert event was like asking for lollipops in a candy store. Three flasks and a can of beer materialized before him. Matt took a silver flask from the most reputable-looking person in the lot and unscrewed the lid.

He slid his arm beneath Kylie's head and hoisted her up. "Take a swig of this just to stop the shaking."

She opened her mouth and he poured a splash onto her tongue. She swallowed and choked, which was the perfect response.

"Who was in charge of those lights?" Harlan Sloan loomed above them on the stage, angry sparks shooting from his light-colored eyes. "We can't afford mistakes like that at this show, especially this show."

One of the workers stepped forward. "I put the lights up there, Mr. Sloan, but they were secure. I made sure of that."

"Not secure enough." He spun around and leveled a finger at the rest of the workers gathered onstage. "If you're not ready to put up the lights, leave them on the ground."

He crouched on the edge of the stage. "Are you all right, Ms. Grant? Do we need to get an ambulance out here?"

Struggling to sit upright, Kylie found her voice. "I'm fine. Nothing hit me. Matt got there just in time."

"I apologize." Sloan jumped to his feet and swept an expansive arm in front of him. "If you're not a paid worker with workers' comp, get off the stage."

The young people who had come to help out grumbled and shot dirty looks at Kylie as if it were her fault a light almost beaned her.

Matt handed the flask of whiskey back to the roadie and kneeled beside Kylie. "Feeling better?"

"At least my hands stopped shaking." She held her hands in front of her. "Don't know if I can say the same about my knees."

"Didn't you see the lights falling?" He pushed up and extended a hand to her. He felt like hauling her to her feet and wrapping his arms around her.

She took his hand, stood up and promptly

swayed, which gave him a good excuse to put his arm around her shoulders. So he did.

"I saw and heard them coming down, but my feet wouldn't budge. I never thought I'd be one of those people too petrified to move out of the way of danger."

"You never know how you're going to react in any situation." Matt jerked his head toward Sloan, still directing traffic. "Did you get a load of how mad Sloan was? He doesn't want any more trouble."

"He doesn't want any trouble at all."

A tremble rolled through her body, and Matt pulled her closer. "What's wrong?"

She put her finger to her lips. "Not here. Let's go back to the bike."

They tromped through the underbrush and Kylie seemed to have regained her sea legs. When they reached his motorcycle, she looked both ways and wedged her shoulder against the nearest tree.

"Don't you think it's kind of a coincidence that we come snooping around the concert site and a huge light nearly falls on my head?"

Matt sucked in the inside of his cheek. He'd been too alarmed at the accident and then too relieved at Kylie's escape to think much about it.

"I suppose so. What do you think?"

"I think Harlan Sloan somehow arranged that accident."

"And you know that…"

"No, I didn't read his mind or anything, Matt. It's just a hunch. The man is oily."

A twig snapped and Matt jumped.

"What is it?" Kylie's face grew even paler.

He mimicked her gesture from before and put his finger to his lips. He crept back toward the underbrush, his motorcycle boots crushing and cracking the wooded carpet beneath him. He pulled back a branch and peered onto the shaded path leading back toward the concert grounds.

"Anyone there?" The hairs on the back of his neck quivered. He could sense a presence, or maybe he'd been hanging out with fortune-tellers too long.

Kylie touched his back and he jumped again. She definitely moved with more stealth than he did.

"Sorry. What did you see?"

"I didn't see anything. Thought I heard someone."

"Could be people coming back to their cars."

He raised one eyebrow. "What were you just saying about coincidences?"

"Let's get out of here."

As they took the winding road away from the concert grounds, Matt leaned into the turns just to feel Kylie tighten her grip around his waist. With her body snug against his back, he could ride all day, straddling his bike while she straddled him.

He slowed down for a bump in the road. He didn't want to flip her off the bike. She'd had enough accidents since landing in Coral Cove.

Were her instincts right about those lights? He couldn't see Sloan clambering among the scaffolding and tipping a set of klieg lights overboard. Was there someone else watching? Someone else who knew their mission...and wanted to make sure it failed?

When he turned his bike onto the Coast Highway, the cool wind hit his face, slapping some sense into him. The lights had to be an accident. The person who took Bree might not even be in the area anymore. He could've been a drifter, someone who targeted these kinds of events looking for naive young women.

Kylie snuggled in closer and Matt eased off the accelerator. No need to rush. No need to get a ticket or put Kylie's life in danger.

When he pulled up to the hotel, Kylie slid off the bike clutching her thin sweater around her. "It gets cold on that thing."

"I didn't notice."

"Maybe because you have that big machine between your legs." She stopped and her face reddened right up to the roots of her black hair.

Matt crossed his arms and grinned.

"I—I mean the bike is warmer when your legs are wrapped around…. I'm just going to stop now."

"Don't stop on my account."

She punched him in the arm and he flexed his biceps just to show her he had more than a big machine between his legs.

"I'm still rattled from that…accident at the concert grounds."

"Sloan wasn't crawling among the scaffolding." He opened the front door of the hotel for Kylie and waved at the front desk clerk. "I think someone would've noticed him."

She turned to him at the elevator. "What did you find out, anyway? We never got a chance to exchange info."

"Not much." He punched the elevator button. "I was talking to the roadies. A few of them were working the gig three years ago and remembered Bree's disappearance, but they couldn't tell me anything, or wouldn't. They're a close-knit bunch. What about you?"

The elevator car settled on the lobby floor with a swoosh.

"I spoke to a trio of young women, girls really. Two of them were clueless about Bree and the other one's mother had told her about Bree as a cautionary tale. They didn't seem too concerned, but I got the feeling one of the primary reasons people come to these concerts is to hook up."

Matt slapped the button for the third floor and said, "News flash."

"I guess I knew that." Kylie settled her back against the wall of the elevator, her palms flat against the fake wood. "I just didn't realize how naive young women could be."

"Were you?" In high school, Kylie had seemed cool, tough, not caring what anyone thought of her—definitely not naive. His clunky high school boy lines would've never worked on her. Not that he'd ever tried…and for the life of him, as she stood in front of him with her wild, dark hair and witchy green eyes, he couldn't figure out why he hadn't.

"Oh, I suppose I was naive, but I had this extrasensory stuff going on, which heightened my awareness more. And my mom always added her own warnings."

"Didn't know about Mr. Brunswick, our resident serial killer, did you? Because apparently, the murders this summer weren't his first."

"You know," she said as she stepped through the doors first and smacked her hand against one side to hold it open for him, "I know you're not going to believe me now, but I always knew there was something off about Mr. Brunswick."

"Besides being sort of handsy with the girls?"

"Yeah, besides that because he never tried any of that stuff with me."

"You probably scared him."

She tilted her head when she reached her door. "Did I scare you back then, too?"

Was she asking him why he never went out with her? Since he'd gone out with about half of the girls in their class.

Should he tell her the truth that a slightly pudgy girl with black hair and blacker eyeliner and bangles halfway up her arms hadn't interested him in the slightest? Kylie and her clique had *outsider* written all over them. He couldn't afford the stench of loser. His father the drunk had already tainted him with that odor.

"Yeah, you scared me."

She flicked her card under his nose. "Liar."

He blocked her entrance with his arm. "Dinner at seven at Burgers and Brews? I've got my camera all ready to hand off to Annie."

"You know where to find me. I'm going to lie down." She massaged her left temple. "My head hurts."

"Just think what it would've felt like if those lights had landed on you." He pinched her chin to make up for not wanting her in high school.

Her lashes dropped and a small sigh from her lips warmed his fingertips. "I never even thanked you for saving my life…again."

"You can thank me later." Her eyes widened and he continued, slapping a serious look on his face. "When you use your super-duper powers to get to the bottom of this mystery and make me look good in the process."

She nodded and shut the door in his face.

Idiot. Kylie leaned her forehead against the door and banged it once, which didn't do her headache any good. At least she hadn't remarked on the big, *hot* machine between his legs.

She tossed her purse onto the bed and cocked her head at the noises coming from Matt's room. Great. He was in the shower…naked. As if she didn't have enough trouble keeping her mind out of the gutter when it came to thoughts about Matt Conner.

It was as if she'd traveled in a time machine right back to high school when she would secretly drool over Matt, who didn't know she was alive. Okay, it wasn't exactly the same. Matt noticed her now—of course, she'd shed a few pounds and lost the creepy makeup.

Which made the situation worse.

Mr. and Mrs. Harris had hired them in good faith to find out what had happened to Bree. The Harrises weren't paying them to brush against each other and utter double entendres. Not that she'd meant that remark as a double entendre.

Who was she kidding?

She'd just spent twenty minutes on the back of his…machine hugging the life out of him. And the fact that the man kept saving her life every ten minutes didn't help. Who knew Matt was so chivalrous? She always figured him for a horny teenager, a horny, hot teenager who'd become a hotter man.

She fell back on the bed and toed off her sneakers. Wiggling her toes, she closed her eyes and breathed deeply through her nose.

The stress of the accident had made her head pound. Other things made her head pound, too—sensitivities, heightened awareness. She'd have to take advantage of her state this time instead of squandering it on her personal quest.

Although…Bree had gone to see Kylie's mother before the young woman had disappeared. Kylie could feel that down to her bones, and once she and Matt got their hands on that police report they could prove it.

She reached for her purse. Fumbling inside, she closed her fingers around a small bottle of ibuprofen. She popped two into her mouth and grabbed the half-full glass of water she'd left on the bedside table, which the hotel maid had left alone. She downed the pills and scooted up to rest her head on a pillow.

Her head sank into the goose-down pillow covered with a freshly laundered pillowcase. She didn't have to close her eyelids. A liquid lethargy seeped into her body, tugging her lids down.

Sleep stole over her like a thief on silent feet and her breathing deepened.

The young woman held out her hand, palm up. "Can you tell my fortune?"

The woman with the gray-streaked black hair, still thick and full, smiled sadly. "It doesn't work that way." Still the young woman thrust out her hand.

"What do you see?"

The older woman tilted her head and took the woman's hand in hers. "You must be careful in matters of the heart. There is one who wants you for selfish reasons." The woman dropped the girl's hand.

"What is it? What do you see?"

The woman shook her head, wisps of gray hair coming loose from her chignon. "Guard your heart, just as all young women must do.

"Guard your heart from a selfish love."

Kylie jolted awake. She knew. Mom had seen Bree's danger.

She squeezed her eyes closed and pinched the bridge of her nose. Was that really Bree? Mom could've been warning anyone…even her own daughter. God knows, she'd suffered through her share of Mom's warnings.

A knock at the door between her room and

Matt's banished the remaining clouds of sleep from her brain. She glanced at the alarm clock—six o'clock already.

She cleared her throat and wiped the back of her hand across her lips. "Yeah?"

"Just wanted to make sure you're awake. I didn't hear a shower running from over here."

Had he been listening for her shower?

"Just woke up. I'll be ready in less than forty-five minutes." It was longer than she usually took to get ready but if Matt was going to do any comparing between her and Annie, she wanted to make sure she wound up on top.

"Take your time. I have a little work to do on my laptop."

Work that didn't involve her? Maybe Mom had been directing her warning to Kylie and not Bree. What did she really know about Matt's life anyway? She'd never been able to pin him down about his cases or his success rate or even where he currently lived. He'd been evasive.

Maybe all this partner business and his interest in the way she worked was just a cover.

Matt rapped on the door again. "You okay?"

"I'm fine. See you in forty-five."

Whatever Matt's intentions, she planned to play along. If he was using her, she could use him, too.

About a half hour later, she leaned into the bathroom mirror to line her eyes with smudgy kohl. She'd learned to use a lighter hand with her makeup over the years, and as far she knew wasn't scaring anyone off anymore.

She tucked the pencil into her makeup bag and finished off with a pink lipstick, since someone had stolen her red. She pressed her fingers against the glass. Had the same person who'd broken into her hotel room shoved that set of lights off the scaffolding?

She glanced over her shoulder. How had he gotten in here anyway? He wouldn't try it again—not with Matt right next door.

She tapped at the adjoining door and clicked the dead bolt. "I'm ready."

As if he'd been waiting with his hand on the doorknob, Matt flung open the door. His dark eyes widened and then grew darker as his gaze swept from her head to her high-heeled sandals.

"You look great."

"Thanks. So do you." He'd swapped his scruffy pair of jeans for a darker pair that flared over his motorcycle boots. His dark blue V-neck shirt hugged his muscled torso in all the right places, and his close-cropped dark hair set off his broad cheekbones.

"We're not taking the bike tonight." She gestured toward her strappy heels.

"Wouldn't want to mess up that perfect mane of hair you have."

She scooped her keys out of her purse and jingled them. "Then I'll drive."

"We could always walk."

"Not in these heels." Besides, she had a plan for later tonight and she'd need her car to carry it out.

They slipped out the front door of the hotel and Kylie threw her sweater over her shoulders. Although the days were mostly sunny and warm at this time of the summer, the nights cooled down with the moist air from the ocean and the wisps of mist that floated in from the water.

She beeped the door open for Matt and they drove the short distance to Coral Cove's main street, already bustling with tourists dining out and hitting the shops for such necessities as sunscreen, foam coolers and air mattresses.

Kylie pulled onto a side street and cut the engine. "So what's the plan for getting the camera to Annie?"

Matt withdrew a small, flat device from his pocket and held it out in the palm of his hand. "We're having dinner, and I see an old friend. I go over to her table, give her a hug and slip the camera in her pocket. She'll be expecting it."

"Sounds good." They exited the car and stepped onto the curb. "Have you seen many old friends since you've been back?"

"A few. I guess a lot of people stuck around. Most of the guys I hung out with took off though."

"Are you sure they aren't in jail?"

"That's funny. And how about your clique? Are they scribbling poetry in some coffeehouse... wearing berets?"

She laughed. "Probably, although I heard one of them is a stockbroker on Wall Street."

"Sellout." He shoved open the door to Burgers and Brews and the noise washed over them.

Kylie whistled. "Glad Annie chose this place for dinner. It's so busy, I don't think anyone would notice if you stood up, yelled across the room and tossed the camera to her."

"I think you're right, but I'll stick to my previous plan."

They had to wait ten minutes for a table, but they'd shown up fifteen minutes early and there was no sign of Annie. The hostess showed them to a table in the middle of the room.

Matt took a seat with his back to the door. "You can watch for Annie. I don't want to give myself away. You remember what she looks like?"

"I can probably figure it out unless she's gained a hundred pounds."

"Nope she looks the same, a few more lines on her face like the rest of us."

Yeah, right. Matt looked better than ever, lines or no.

They ordered a couple of beers and cheeseburgers from the waiter and acted like any other couple on a date.

Kylie took a sip of her beer and glanced up as the door to the restaurant swung open for about the fiftieth time since they sat down. But this time their quarry stood in the entrance, smoothing her summer dress along her slim hips.

Annie Summerholdt had the same figure she'd had in high school—a pretty girl had turned into a pretty woman. Kylie bit her lip when the waiter placed her towering cheeseburger and mass of onion rings in front of her. She puffed out a breath and grabbed the ketchup. She wasn't in competition with Annie. Besides, Matt seemed to appreciate her curves.

She flipped the bun off her burger and aimed a stream of ketchup onto the bread. "Bingo."

"What?" Matt had been busy dressing up his own burger.

"Our accomplice just entered the building."

"Good, about bloody time, too." He dropped a slice of tomato on his burger and licked his fingers. "I'll take a trip to the bathroom in a few minutes, spot my old high school friend on the way back to our table and pop over to say hello."

Kylie tipped her head at the empty table next to them. "I hope they don't put her there. That could be awkward."

"That's a table for four. I don't think the hostess

will put her there. Annie implied she was coming over for a bite to eat on her own. She's friends with Bryan, the owner, so she just might sit at the bar."

"Nope." Kylie narrowed her eyes as the hostess led Annie to a cozy table for two in the corner. "She's sitting at a table near the front. Should be easy for you to notice her on your way out of the men's room."

"Great." Matt took a bite of his cheeseburger and wiped his face with his napkin while he chewed.

"Where's the document camera?"

"In my pocket." He patted the breast pocket of his faded denim shirt that he'd pulled on over his shirt. "I'll conceal it in my hand and slip it into hers when we shake."

"What are you waiting for?"

He glanced at his plate. "I'm hungry."

"You can eat after you deliver the goods."

"Are you trying to talk like a P.I.?"

"Go!"

Shaking his head he plucked the napkin from his lap and dropped it next to his plate. "Do *not* steal any of my food."

Two bright red spots popped up on Kylie's cheeks. "I have my own food. Does it look like I could eat yours, too?"

He hunched over the table and whispered, "After what you've been through the past few days, you could use it to keep up your strength. So help yourself."

"I think I'm good." She crunched into an onion ring and made shooing motions with her hands.

Matt skirted through the tables on his way to the bathroom. He had to watch his jokes around Kylie. Why was she so sensitive about her appearance? She wasn't a chubby teenager anymore. The woman had curves in all the right places.

Matt grabbed a couple of paper towels and wiped his hands. Besides being overly sensitive, Kylie had kind of a weird vibe about her tonight. She'd smiled and said all the right things, but she had a faraway look in her green eyes.

That's what he'd remembered about her in high school—untouchable, aloof. But he didn't want that from her now, dammit. He wanted her…any way he could get her.

He couldn't believe he was contemplating mixing business with pleasure again. That combustible combination had blindsided him before. At his age, he should've learned by now how to control his animal urges when he stumbled on a pretty woman.

But Kylie was more than a pretty woman. She plucked all his strings.

He snorted and tossed the paper towel in the trash can. He'd tell himself just about anything to bed a woman he wanted.

He scooped the small camera from his pocket

and slipped it into the palm of his hand. Nobody would be watching two old high school friends get reacquainted anyway. He was probably carrying this spy stuff a little too far, but then what did he know about being a P.I.?

This was his first case.

He ambled out of the men's room and into the dining room. He zeroed in on his table first, and Kylie smiled an encouraging sort of smile. Was he acting nervous?

He looked past Kylie at Annie, sipping a glass of wine and staring out the window. He made his way to her table, and she glanced up at his approach, lines of worry creasing her forehead.

His gut rolled. Was he putting her in danger with his request? He could find another way. Hell, he'd break into the files himself if he had to.

He forced a grin to his lips. "Annie Summer-holdt. Long time, no see."

He extended his hand, and as she stood up to greet him he pulled her close with the other arm and whispered in her ear. "You don't have to do this."

Her cool hand closed around his and she took the camera from him. She dipped her hand in the pocket of her sweater and the camera disappeared. "It's great to see you, Matt. Are you in town long?"

"Not too long."

They exchanged inane chatter for a few minutes, but he got the feeling Annie wanted him to go away…fast.

"I'm glad I ran into you. Take care." He extended his hand again, but she stood on tiptoe to kiss his cheek.

Her lips brushed his ear. "I tried to warn you, Matt. Don't worry. Now get out of here."

He smiled and backed away from her table. Was there some mysterious force at work on the women of Coral Cove tonight making them jumpy, sensitive and weird?

He made his way from one moody female to another and dropped into his chair across from Kylie, blowing out a breath.

"Well? Everything go okay? You look strange."

"I'm not the strange one around here." He took a swig of beer. "Annie took the camera but she was talking about warning me and telling me to get away from her table."

Kylie's mouth dropped open as she gazed past his shoulder.

Now what? He had no intention of turning around. The look of horror on Kylie's face meant *someone* had to keep it together.

"What's wrong?"

"Don't turn around."

Matt knocked his fork to the ground and bent forward to pick it up. While under the table, he swiveled his head toward Annie's table and nearly fell over headfirst.

Pulling out a chair at the table of the woman who'd just told him not to worry was the man Matt worried about the most—the police chief of Coral Cove.

Chapter Eight

Matt bumped his head on the table on the way up and cursed.

"That's what I say." Kylie was gripping the edge of the table. "What is your mole doing with the enemy?"

"Looks like they're having dinner."

"She set you up, Matt."

"Hold on." He gripped both sides of the table with his hands.

"Maybe that's what Annie was going to warn me about."

"About being in cahoots with Chief Evans?"

"I don't think she is." Matt drained the rest of his beer. "Think about it. We made arrangements to meet here. She must've been planning to come here on her own and then the chief invited himself along."

Kylie started shaking her head and Matt put a finger to her lips.

"Annie looked worried when I approached. She wanted to get rid of me before Evans arrived."

"I don't know, Matt. I don't like it."

"I'm going to trust her, Kylie." Would he live to regret it, just like the last time he decided to trust a woman?

She shoved her half-eaten cheeseburger to the center of the table. "I'm going to make sure you can."

Then Matt saw what Kylie had seen. Annie was weaving through the tables on her way to the restrooms.

"You're going to corner her in the bathroom?"

"Yep." She pushed back from the table and was gone in a swirl of skirts.

Annie was in for it now.

Kylie pushed through the ladies' room and parked herself in front of the vanity. She ran the water and leaned toward the mirror to inspect her makeup.

She darted a glance at the bathroom door and clicked the lock. She'd rather get a few patrons mad at the locked bathroom than have anyone overhear her conversation with Annie.

Annie came out of the stall and stumbled to a stop. "You're with Matt, aren't you?"

Before Kylie had time to relish the sound of that, she responded. "I'm working the Harris case with him. We really need that police file. Are you going to rat him out to Evans?"

Annie pushed past her and stuck her hands beneath the automatic faucet. "I wouldn't do that to Matt. He saved my life."

"What are you doing with Evans?"

Annie met Kylie's eyes in the mirror. "Having dinner. Look, I may not approve of the way the man conducts police business, but we've been out a few times and he's not a bad guy."

"Like Dave Kenner wasn't a bad guy?"

Annie dropped her lashes and soaped up her hands. "Don't be so superior, Kylie. You didn't have the same issues in high school as us mortal girls."

Kylie clenched her jaw to stop it from dropping to her chest. Was Annie delusional?

"You and your oh-so-cool clique of artsy friends didn't care what anyone thought of you. You laughed at the rest of us for caring about prom and football games."

She and her friends *did* laugh at the pursuits of the other students—only because they were jealous. Or at least she was.

Annie grabbed for a paper towel. "The rest of us were worried about acceptance and fitting in. I dated Dave to be in the popular crowd and found out later I had to pay a high price—until Matt rescued me."

"So you're going to snap pictures of that police report?"

Someone tried the door handle and then pounded on the door. "Hey, this isn't supposed to be locked."

"I told Matt I'd do it and I will. Brett…the chief called me after I spoke to Matt and wouldn't take no for an answer for a dinner date. I gave the chief a later meeting time so I could get the camera from Matt. I'm going to do it, Kylie."

The door rattled again, and Kylie moved in closer to Annie and whispered, "You'd better not double-cross Matt."

She flung open the door, confronting a scowling woman. "Sorry. I didn't realize I'd locked it."

She breezed out of the bathroom and flopped into her chair. "Okay, I guess we're just going to have to trust her."

"Did she convince you in there?"

"How can you ever be sure? But I guess we have to trust her. She has the camera now. She's either going to do it or tell Brett."

"Brett?"

"That's Chief Evans to you and me. They're dating, apparently."

Matt leaned back in his chair and crossed his arms. "Is she ever going to learn?"

"You don't think Evans is abusive, do you?"

"I don't know. He seems the type—power hungry, arrogant."

"Well, that's not our problem now. I just hope she comes through for you."

"For us." Matt covered her hand with his.

Kylie snorted. "I don't flatter myself that she's doing anything for me."

Matt brushed his hands together. "It's a done deal now. Are you going to finish those onion rings?"

"Help yourself, but we need to get going."

"We do?"

"I need to get going. There's something I have to do."

"Now? Tonight?"

She avoided his searching eyes by plowing through her purse. "Uh-huh."

"Are you going to tell me?" He gestured to the waiter. "Check, please."

"I'm going back to the concert grounds."

"What?"

"I'm ready, Matt." She wound her hair around one hand and tossed it over her shoulder. "I had a dream about my mother, but I think she was talking to Bree this time. She knew something, sensed danger around Bree."

"Kylie, it's not safe to go back there, especially after what happened this afternoon."

She arched one eyebrow. "Now you're admitting that it might not have been an accident?"

"Why take chances? Who knows what's going on at the concert grounds tonight?"

"You afraid there might be a wild orgy?"

"That would be the least of your worries. Why can't you get in touch with Bree in your hotel room?"

"Because Bree wasn't in my hotel room. She was at the concert. It's better."

"Then I'm coming with you."

"I—I'd like that. Sometimes…" She stopped. She'd never let anyone in on the secrets of her profession. She'd always been afraid that it would dilute her power. That belief had isolated her over the years.

"Sometimes what?"

She pressed her fingertips to her eyelids. "Sometimes when I have a vision or a communication, it weakens me. In the end, I believe that's why my mother killed herself. She wasn't as good at filtering as I am. The sensations would bombard her unbidden. She never knew which world she inhabited half the time."

"Then let me be there for you, Kylie. This is dangerous stuff. You shouldn't be alone."

She didn't want to be alone. For the first time in a long time, she didn't want to be alone.

She stabbed a finger at the check. "Then whip

out some of that expense account money and pay the bill."

As they left the restaurant, Kylie glanced at Annie and Chief Evans laughing and sharing a dessert.

She couldn't blame Annie. A girl deserved a warm body now and then.

"I suppose you need to change clothes again. You're not going to go traipsing about in the wilderness with those shoes."

"It's hardly the wilderness."

Matt opened the car door for her. "Oh, I don't know. Have you ever been out there by yourself? No lights, no other people, just you and the coyotes."

Kylie shivered before sliding into the seat of the car. "When you put it that way."

They both changed clothes and got back into Kylie's car.

"Do you think anyone's going to be there?" Kylie clenched the steering wheel with clammy hands as she accelerated onto the highway.

"Probably. The concert opens in a few days. Even if the crew isn't working around the clock, there's bound to be some of them staying on-site. Didn't you see the trailers behind the stage?"

"I didn't notice." She glanced at his profile. "Maybe you can question more people since your investigation sort of got cut off today."

"I don't want to be too far away from you."

She didn't want that either.

"And I don't want to hold up your investigation." She swung the car down the road that cut through the trees and thick foliage. "It doesn't seem like you're getting anywhere since you have to stop and rescue me every hour on the hour."

Losing reception, the radio crackled and hissed and Matt fiddled with the buttons. "I'm waiting for that police report. It will give me something to investigate. Mr. Harris didn't know much about his daughter's activities down here, and I don't think he ever requested to read the police report—too painful I guess."

"I had the same problem with Mrs. Harris. She seemed to think I could just come down here with her daughter's scarf and Bree would communicate with me and tell me what happened."

Matt snapped his fingers. "And it doesn't work that way."

Kylie parked the car in a clearing next to two other cars and turned to Matt. "You don't seem concerned about Annie and Chief Evans."

"Call me an idiot, but I trust her."

"I suppose the worst she could do at this point is tell the chief. It means we'd never get our hands on the report, but it would end there."

"She's not going to tell the chief and this time

tomorrow night, we'll be reading the police report."

Kylie envied Matt his confidence. Maybe it had something to do with growing up independent and self-reliant. Matt Conner had always been his own boss...even at thirteen. His trust in his fellow man surprised her, given the number of times the adults in Matt's life had let him down.

She stepped out of the car and inhaled the mingled scents of the ocean and pine needles. She had to hand it to Sloan. He'd picked a great place for an outdoor concert—too bad he couldn't guarantee the safety of the concertgoers.

Matt stretched and cupped a hand to his ear. "Sounds like we have company."

Rock music floated on the air and an occasional shout of laughter pierced the calm night.

"Roadies partying?"

"Wouldn't be the first time." Matt parted two branches. "Come on. I'll lead the way."

They trampled through the underbrush again and peered between leaves at the bowl, still buzzing with activity. The hordes from earlier in the day had thinned, but a dedicated bunch clustered around the stage, while a radio blared and a cloud of smoke floated above them.

"Looks like there's more relaxing than working going on." Matt jerked his thumb at the group.

"And those better be legal cigarettes they're smoking."

Wrinkling her nose, Kylie said, "Even if they're not, you can't exactly arrest them. You're a P.I., not a cop."

Matt sucked in sharp breath. "So I am. Looks like a good opportunity to ask some questions. Can your...um...séance wait?"

"Since it's not a séance, yeah." She ducked under the branches into the clearing. "Let's go talk to some roadies."

One by one, the people on the stage turned their faces toward them as they approached. Kylie tucked her hand in the crook of Matt's arm.

A man sitting in the middle of the group, his legs dangling over the side, raised a tattooed arm and pointed at Kylie. "Hey, you're the one who almost got knocked out by those klieg lights."

"That's me."

"Sorry 'bout that. That was Roger's fault." He pushed the man next to him.

Roger flicked his cigarette into the dirt at the foot of the stage. "No way, man. I secured those lights on the scaffolding. I don't know how they came loose."

Matt crushed the glowing cigarette butt with his boot. "We were here today to get some information about a girl who disappeared from this event three years ago. Bree Harris? Ever hear of her?"

The tattooed man nodded. "I didn't know her name, but I was working that gig then, and we were real upset when we heard."

"Did you hear any rumors at the time about it? Had she hooked up with someone?" Matt shoved his hands in his pockets and propped his foot on a chair.

"A lot of people hook up here." A short man with a shaved head draped his arms around the woman next to him and she squeezed his thigh.

"They'd know better than us." Roger jerked his thumb toward a group of men lounging on the other side of the stage drinking beers. "Those are the local boys. When this show ended, we packed up and beat it."

"Did the Coral Cove cops ask you any questions?"

"A few, but I think they were happy to see us go."

Matt slipped a batch of cards out of his pocket and handed them around. "I'm investigating the case for the parents. If you remember anything, give me a call."

Matt took Kylie's arm. "One more stop and you can get busy."

The young men stopped laughing when Matt approached. He looked intimidating with his black leather jacket and motorcycle boots. The C.C.P.D.

must've been happy that he'd landed on the right side of the law.

"How are you boys doing tonight?"

They mumbled their answers, and one blond with an angelic face asked, "Can we help you with something?"

Matt flicked out another card. "I'm a private investigator looking into the cold case of a missing woman. She disappeared from this concert three years ago, and her parents want some answers."

The blond took the card and passed it to his buddies. "Yeah, I remember that."

The young man next to him whistled. "I do, too. Her name was Bree, but she wasn't a local. Hung out here for a few days before the concert."

Matt swept his arm across the four of them. "Were you all working back then, too?"

Three out of the four young men, including the blond and the guy next to him with the buzz cut, said they'd worked that concert, too.

Kylie pulled a notepad out of her purse and handed it to the first guy on the left. "Would you mind writing down your names and numbers in case we want to talk to you again?"

The blond swung his legs nervously and glanced at his friend, but Buzz Cut held out his hand. "Sure. I can't tell you anything more though. She was hanging out with some of the local girls, so you might want to talk to them."

"We will." *As soon as we get that police report with all their names unredacted.*

They handed the notepad down the line until it reached the last guy, who held up his hands. "I wasn't even living here then."

"That's okay then." Kylie took back the notebook and glanced at the names: Kenny Durrell had the buzz cut, Toby Reynolds was the blond and Rob Kauffman was the quiet one. Would they find any of these names in the police report? Would they ever get their hands on the police report?

"Thanks, guys." Matt cupped her elbow and steered her away from the stage. "Good work, detective."

"What, the notepad?" She smacked it against her hand. "I'm not just about channeling vibes, you know. I've worked pretty closely with the police. I imagine you have to do your own legwork. I don't think cops appreciate P.I.'s much, do they?"

"Nope." He spun her around to face him and rested his hands on her shoulders. "Where do you plan to…try to reach Bree?"

"It can be anywhere, but I need quiet." Her gaze swept the bowl and she pointed to a spot on the edge, next to a clump of trees. "There."

The big lights ringing the stage blinked off one by one. Knots of people drifted away, and the roadies headed back to their trailers.

Matt flicked on his flashlight. "I wonder if the locals sleep out here?"

Kylie glanced over her shoulder at the darkened stage where shadows flitted into the night. "Looks like everyone is taking off."

When they reached the spot Kylie had picked, Matt propped his boot on a log. "Will this work?"

"Perfect." Kylie dipped her hand into the pocket of her jacket and pulled out Bree's scarf. The fluid material felt alive in her hands.

As she began to lower herself onto the log, Matt said, "Wait."

He slipped out of his jacket and spread it on the log for her. "Might as well get comfortable."

The worn leather creaked as she settled on the jacket. She stuck her legs in front of her and leaned against the tree behind the log.

Matt turned his back to her as if she were about to practice some magic and he didn't want to learn her secrets.

She held the scarf in her hands, the silky folds cascading across her skin. She closed her eyes. *Are you here, Bree?*

A light breeze toyed with the ends of Kylie's hair and the scent of fresh lemons teased her nose. Her lashes fluttered, but she couldn't raise her eyelids. She'd lost the sense of Matt's presence. The night closed in on her, isolating her. She was alone in the world.

No. Not quite alone.

She whispered aloud. "Bree?"

A chill crept over Kylie's flesh. So cold. So alone.

A swirl of emotions cascaded through her body. Happiness. Confusion. Anger. Fear.

The feelings, like a wave, swept her along a zigzag course. Kylie tried to keep her head above the water. Tried to snatch onto a stationary branch as she rushed by. Tried to discern some kernel of truth amid the jumble of sensations. Tried to grab something solid.

Then the terror sliced through her. She tried to filter, but fear overwhelmed her.

Run, Bree, run.

Her feet were rooted to the ground. Her fate sealed.

Kylie reached out a hand to touch Bree. She was so close. Why couldn't Bree just lean over and whisper in her ear? Why couldn't she identify her killer?

Close, so close.

Kylie gasped and her lids flew open. She was here.

Bree was in Coral Cove.

Chapter Nine

Matt wiped his sweaty palms on his jeans. Was Kylie awake? Out of her trance?

It had taken incredible willpower for him not to rush over to that log and shake her out of whatever weird nightmare had her in its grip. She had slumped against the tree behind her, eyes closed, lids twitching, mouth working, a cavalcade of emotions sweeping across her face.

She'd opened her eyes, but her gaze wasn't focused—not focused on anything in this world anyway. A soft moan escaped her lips.

Matt took one step forward. "Kylie?"

Her face crumpled in what looked like pain and her eyelids fluttered.

Matt plowed forward and dropped to his knees beside her. He took both of her cold hands in his and rubbed them. "Are you okay? Do you need anything?"

Her green eyes wandered to his face. She blinked

a few more times and the haziness cleared. The green darkened.

"Matt." She bunched the T-shirt covering his chest in her fists. "Bree's here."

"Here?" He swiveled his head around, expecting to see a ghost floating out of the trees. "What do you mean, she's here?"

She snatched one hand away from him and pressed a palm to her forehead. "I—I'm not sure. She's here in Coral Cove. I felt her here, close by."

Matt sucked the inside of his cheek between his teeth and measured his words before blurting them out. Hell, he didn't know how all this worked. "Did she tell you this? Did she name her killer?"

The hand slipped and Kylie covered her eyes. "No, no. She's not going to stand before me and talk. I just felt her near me. She's still here in Coral Cove."

Matt sat back on his heels. "Do you mean her body? Her body is in Coral Cove?"

"I guess so." She clamped her hands between her bouncing knees. "She must be dead, Matt, but then we both figured that, right?"

"I think the Harrises might still be holding out hope, but yeah, I figured they were sending me on a murder investigation whether or not they wanted to admit it."

"Her murder is tied into this concert."

"And if a stranger killed her, some guy hitching

on to this concert for an opportunity to be around a lot of free-spirited young women not taking normal precautions, we're going to have a tough time identifying him."

"I know." She wound her hair into a loose bun, tying it like a knot. "But the police never even got that far. It's as if they wanted to shove the whole incident under the carpet."

"Of course they did. If they didn't have any easy clues to solve the case, they'd want to get it out of the public's consciousness as quickly as possible, especially with no body."

"Then they could pass it off as a runaway."

"Exactly." Several strands of Kylie's hair had escaped her makeshift bun, and Matt swept them off her face with his finger. "How do you feel?"

"Disappointed. I didn't get as much information as I thought I would." She splayed her hands in front of her. "It was all so confusing, jumbled."

He rolled his eyes. "I meant, how do you feel physically? I can tell you, that trance stuff is no fun to watch."

"I'm a little weak." Hunching her shoulders, she crossed her arms. "I felt Bree's fear. It's debilitating. I just wish I could've discovered more, gotten closer to her during the actual murder."

Matt's brows shot up. "That doesn't sound good."

"It's not good for me, but it's good for the victims. That's how I get a lot of my information, through those sensations when the person is close to death."

"Let's get back to the hotel." Matt pushed up from the log and extended his hand. He didn't want to admit to Kylie that her abilities creeped him out. He'd been with people as they took their last breaths, but couldn't imagine being inside their heads.

She grabbed his hand, her fingers curling around his. "I'm sorry. That was too much information, wasn't it?"

Busted. He had to remember she could read minds. He pulled her against his chest and rested his chin on her head. "You just keep doing what you do best. I can handle the details."

She murmured against his shoulder. "I thought you could. I've never much shared what goes on when I go into a trance with anyone, except with my mother. Once she left me…"

Matt hugged her tighter. He'd have to be better about controlling his emotions—not something he'd practiced much.

"You can share it all with me, Kylie. You can trust me."

The underbrush crackled and snapped and Matt and Kylie jumped apart. The four young local men came crashing out of the trees, laughing and pushing at each other. They stumbled to a stop when they saw Matt and Kylie.

"You still here?"

Matt slipped his arm around Kylie's waist. "Just wrapping up."

The guy with the buzz cut, Kenny, pointed across the bowl. "Are you parked in the clearing on the north side? We'll walk with you."

Matt gestured toward a few clumps of sleeping bags around the perimeter of the bowl. "I thought you guys spent the night here."

Toby laughed. "I still live with my mom. She'd kill me if I spent the night out here."

Kenny shrugged. "My parents don't care, especially since they're collecting rent money from me, but these guys are a bunch of wussies."

The quiet one, Rob, punched Kenny in the gut and the other two piled on him. Kylie caught Matt's eye and shook her head. She'd obviously never seen a bunch of guys roughhousing, and these four young men, barely out of boyhood, were no different.

"We're going to get going." With his arm still around Kylie, Matt pulled her as he started walking back to the car.

The locals crashed through the trees behind them and Matt was glad of their company since they'd dispelled the atmosphere around Kylie's communication with Bree. The guys' antics and noise had brought him and Kylie back to earth.

And that's where they needed to be right now.

When they got back to the clearing, Kylie beeped her remote and Matt opened the door for her.

The locals stopped at an older model muscle car and Kenny asked, "Where's your bitchin' bike?"

Matt wedged his hip against Kylie's car and aimed his flashlight at the group. "How'd you know I rode a motorcycle?"

Toby's fair skin flushed. "Ah, we saw you riding it around town."

"Drive carefully." Matt smacked the hood of the car and walked around to the passenger side.

When he shut the door, Kylie cranked on the engine and turned to him. "So they already noticed you."

"They noticed the bike. That's not unusual." He hit his knuckle against the window. "Did you see their car? Do you *hear* their car? They'd notice a bitchin' bike."

"I hope they didn't notice anything else, like my little trip to the other side."

He ran his hand down her denim-clad thigh and squeezed her knee. "Don't worry about it. I've got your back."

Matt felt like he had to keep reassuring Kylie to get her to trust him. His two rescues had gone a long way toward convincing her. Too bad he'd been deceiving her about…other things.

She slammed on the brakes and he lurched forward, straining against his seat belt. "What was that all about?"

"I—I thought I saw an animal in the road." Her white-knuckled hands gripped the steering wheel.

"That's possible out here. Do you want me to take over the driving duties?"

She blew out a long breath and pinned her shoulders to the back of the seat. "No, I'm good, just a little jumpy still. Matt, do you think Bree's body could be buried somewhere here in Coral Cove?"

"Maybe the killer dumped her out to sea."

"Wouldn't her body have washed up along the shoreline?"

"Not necessarily. Not if he took her out on a boat and weighted down her body. She could be lying at the bottom of the ocean."

"It's hard to make a case without a body."

"I've done…it's been done."

"Maybe we won't have to do it this time. Maybe Bree will lead me to her burial place and we'll find evidence with the body."

"We'll have a lot more to work with once we get our hands on that police report." The cell phone in his pocket buzzed and he checked the display. "It's Annie. Maybe some of your telepathic powers are rubbing off on me."

He punched the button to answer the call and put it on speakerphone. "Hello, Annie, how was your dinner?"

"I'm so sorry, Matt. I tried to call you earlier to warn you, but I couldn't reach you."

"I know. I saw the missed calls later. So what's your story, and you're on speakerphone because I'm with Kylie Grant."

"Oh." Annie paused and sighed. "Chief Evans and I have been going out here and there, nothing serious. When he called tonight, I really couldn't get out of it. I made our date after our meeting time, hoping we could take care of business before he arrived. And we did."

"Barely, and you gave me a shock."

"I'm sure Kylie filled you in on our bathroom chat, didn't you, Kylie?"

"I did."

"I told her I'd go through with it, and I will."

They'd pulled into the hotel parking lot by now and Kylie was poking him in the thigh. She whispered, "What does she owe Evans?"

"Kylie wants to know what you owe Chief Evans? Are you going to feel like you're betraying him?"

Annie snorted. "Kylie wants to know? I see I didn't convince her in the bathroom."

"Not completely, but then she's a tough nut to crack."

Kylie punched him in the arm and he grinned. He liked it when she got physical with him.

"She's a nut all right...oh, yeah, we're on speaker. Hello, Kylie."

Kylie snatched the phone out of his hand. "Annie, stop screwing around. This is serious. Can we count on you or not?"

"That's why I called Matt. I wanted to explain what I was doing with the chief. What he and I have going on has nothing to do with helping you out, Matt. I have the camera, I took a couple of practice shots and I'm ready to go tomorrow."

"Don't get caught, Annie."

"I don't intend to. Brett...er...the chief has his morning meeting with the mayor at nine o'clock. I can take care of business then."

"Thanks." Matt winked at Kylie. "When you're ready to drop off the camera, stick it in a manila envelope and run into me at the post office."

"Okay. Around lunchtime?"

"Yeah, if this isn't all too cloak-and-dagger for you."

"I want to help you, Matt, but I don't want to jeopardize things with the chief either, so the more cloak-and-dagger the better." She paused. "He's not ever going to know you have the report, is he?"

Matt glanced at Kylie. "I don't see why he should."

"Then I'll see you at the post office around noon tomorrow."

Chewing her lip, Kylie ended the call for him. "I hope Chief Evans doesn't find out. Aside from the risk to her job, deception is never a great way to start a relationship."

The muscle in Matt's jaw twitched. Usually deception didn't bode well for a relationship, but some things were better kept to yourself. "I didn't get the impression Annie was looking for a happily-ever-after with the chief, did you?"

"I don't know." She shoved open her car door. "A lot of women begin every relationship with the hope of a happy ending."

Matt sat still for a moment. And Kylie Grant? Was she looking for a happy ending?

KYLIE GRIPPED THE DOORJAMB between the two rooms, hers and Matt's. Maybe having Mr. Irresistible right next door wasn't such a great idea... but it sure made her feel safe. Physically safe, that is. All bets were off when it came to her emotional safety.

"I'll be fine. We do not need to leave the door open."

"I'll settle for unlocked."

"Fine. I'll leave the door unlocked, but I promise you won't need to come rushing to my rescue in the middle of the night."

In two long strides Matt stood in front of her, taking her breath away with his nearness, his masculine scent, the dark bristles sprinkled across his chin…and the look in his dark eyes. "I won't mind if I have to."

Was he going to kiss her? She wanted him to, but how should she go about signaling that without putting herself out there? Without putting herself at risk?

He stepped back, a half smile tweaking one side of his mouth. The panic and indecision in her eyes must've driven him away. Wouldn't be the first time she'd had that effect on a man.

"So call me if you wake up from any nightmares or if you have some kind of epiphany—otherworldly or not."

"I already had one epiphany tonight—Bree Harris is somewhere in Coral Cove. Do you believe me?"

"I believe you, Kylie. Now, get some rest."

She snapped the door close between them, and Matt tried the handle. "Just checking."

Hooking her fingers behind her back, Kylie stared at the door. What if she left it open just a crack? What if she did have one of her nightmares? Would he come to her bed?

She spun around and checked the chain on the other door. Nah, she didn't play those cheap games. She didn't play any games at all.

She peered into the mirror, bracing her hands on the vanity. That wasn't exactly true. She'd lead a guy along for a while and then…bam…shut him down. She couldn't give any man that one little extra step into her life—that trust bit.

But having Matt nearby as she'd gone into a trance tonight, trying to communicate with Bree was a huge step. She'd never allowed a man to see her at her most vulnerable. Of course, Matt had already seen her dangling from a landing and dodging a pair of killer lights. What was left?

The next morning Kylie staggered out of bed after a restless night of undefined dreams. She'd left the connecting door unlocked all night, and Matt hadn't made one attempt to check up on her.

Not that she'd needed it.

Although she'd gotten up a few times for water, kicked off the covers and punched her pillow until she'd flattened it, she hadn't cried out for help or even fallen out of bed onto the floor.

She crept to the adjoining door and pressed her ear against it. Silence.

She glanced at the numbers glowing on the alarm clock and realized it was later than she'd thought. Matt must be out and about already, and they hadn't made plans for breakfast.

But they had plans for lunch.

The hotel phone rang and Kylie jumped. "Hello?"

"Do you want to join me downstairs for breakfast?"

Matt's voice, clear and strong, acted like a splash of cold water to her face.

"I figured you were up already when I didn't hear any noises from your room."

"Went for a run. I'm down here at the lobby café sitting at a table for two if you want to join me."

"I'm almost ready." Kylie tugged at the long T-shirt that passed as pajamas. "Give me fifteen minutes."

"You got it. I'm going to grab a local paper and try not to look like a loser eating alone."

As if Matt Conner could ever look like a loser.

"I'll be there in a flash to rescue you from loserdom."

Kylie whipped off her T-shirt and cranked on the shower. After brushing her teeth, she stepped into the warm spray.

She'd never been so eager to work on a case and it had everything to do with Matt. Amazing that just two days ago, his presence had irritated her. Amazing how a pair of soulful dark eyes and a hard body could change everything.

Breathless, Kylie skidded to a stop at the café entrance. She didn't want Matt to think she was rushing on his account. She tightened her messy ponytail and sighed—not that he couldn't tell she'd been rushing.

He spotted her before she could properly catch her breath. A broad grin split his face as he waved her over.

Her disheveled appearance didn't seem to faze him…but his appearance did more than faze her. The faded T-shirt tight across his shoulders and the running shorts exposing his muscled thighs made her weak in the knees. The disheveled look suited him just fine.

He jumped up to pull out the chair across from him. "Sorry for the grunge look. After I ran, I felt like I could eat a side of beef."

She wiggled her fingers toward his single cup of coffee. "You didn't have to wait for me. You could've gotten started on your side of beef."

"That's okay." His glance swept her from messy head to toes shoved in a pair of flip-flops. "You said you were almost ready."

Her cheeks warmed. "I was."

"Rough night?"

"You can tell?" She swept her fingers beneath her eyes.

"Don't worry. You look as fresh as the morning dew."

"Don't patronize me with clichés. I look like hell."

"I heard you popping up and down more times than a jack-in-the-box last night."

"Couldn't sleep, but if you heard me you mustn't have been doing too much sleeping yourself."

"I'm a light sleeper and just wanted to make sure you weren't having nightmares or more visions."

"Just run-of-the-mill insomnia."

"Yeah, fueled by a few freaky accidents." He snapped his fingers. "You'll never guess who our waiter is."

She didn't have to guess. Toby Reynolds, one of the locals from last night approached their table with a shy smile. "Hi, I didn't know you were staying at the hotel."

"We didn't know you worked here."

"Kenny and I work here. He's one of the guys from last night, too."

Matt flipped open his menu. "That will make it easier for you guys to contact us if you hear anything about Bree Harris."

"The professional roadies don't talk much to us, but we'll keep our ears open."

"You do that."

Matt ordered a big breakfast, but Kylie hadn't just run twenty miles or whatever he did so she stuck to some fruit and cereal.

"How are you going to develop the film from that document camera?"

"My laptop." He dumped some cream in the coffee Toby had refreshed. "I'll connect to a USB and we'll be able to read that report this afternoon."

"I wonder what's in there the police don't want us to see."

Matt shrugged. "Just all the evidence they couldn't use to solve the case. They don't want someone stepping in and solving it for them. Makes 'em look bad."

"I can see that, but the fate of a young woman should be more important than the department's reputation."

Matt's eyes darkened and narrowed to slits. "You'd think a lot of things would be more important than a department's reputation."

The tension in Matt's face gave him a hard, uncompromising look. And it reminded Kylie once again that she knew very little about the man.

He'd been private as a boy and that hadn't changed.

A busboy instead of Toby delivered their food and they ate in silence, Matt probably contemplating that report as much as she was. But for different reasons.

Kylie wanted to confirm that Bree had visited her mother before she disappeared. Had her mother sensed something? She must have. She'd been delivering that warning to Bree…and maybe just a little bit to her daughter.

Matt pushed away his empty plate. "I feel almost human. Now all I need is a shower to complete the transformation."

"Do you want me to go to the post office with you?"

"I think I can handle it, but that doesn't mean you should go wandering around Columbella on your own or the concert grounds."

"Which is it, Matt? You either believe my accidents were planned attacks on me or they were just accidents."

"I have no idea at this point, but someone did break into your hotel room and warn you off. That's a fact."

"So now you're saying I'm not safe in my hotel room?"

"You know what?" He pulled a wad of cash from the nylon belt around his waist and shoved it toward her. "Why don't you go to the spa or get your nails done in that blue color. Relax."

Kylie's jaw dropped. "Are you serious? You do the heavy lifting and I'm supposed to veg out at a spa?"

"Kylie." He covered her hand. "You've done enough heavy lifting the past few days. I have selfish reasons. I don't want you to burn out. We're going to need your psychic powers down the road." He thumped his chest. "I feel it here."

"Maybe you have a point, but I can use my own money."

"Remember, I have the expense account."

"You are not putting my massage on the Harris expense account."

"No, it's on me." He pressed a few bills into her hand. "I'd feel a lot better if you were getting pampered instead of threatened."

"Is there any particular reason you want to ditch me for the meeting with Annie?"

He cocked his head. "Is that what you call leaving you in the capable hands of a masseuse?"

"Don't get me wrong. I appreciate the gesture."

"Then accept it and relax. It will look more natural if I head to the post office myself, less like we're on the case if I'm alone. Besides, I actually do have to go to the post office…and I do have some business to take care of."

Business he didn't want her to know about? Kylie bit her lip. Even after two rescues, she still couldn't cut the guy a break.

She swept the bills from the table. "All right then. I accept. Annie doesn't like me much anyway."

He shrugged. "Just jealous."

"Can I take this?" Toby had approached their table and pointed to the money on the silver tray.

"Yeah, it's all there."

Toby's hand hovered over the check and his blue eyes met Kylie's. "I didn't tell you last night, but

I'd met that girl when she was here for the concert."

"Did you get to know her at all?"

"Not really. She seemed nice, you know, just
here for a good time like everyone else."

Matt raised his brows. "Why didn't you tell us
that last night?"

A dark scowl had claimed Matt's face and Kylie
didn't want him to scare off Toby. She aimed an
encouraging smile at Toby's face. "Thanks for telling us. You'll let us know if you remember anything else about her, right?"

"A-absolutely." He stumbled away clutching the
tray.

Matt's eyes narrowed as they followed Toby
back to the register behind the counter. "He didn't
answer the question."

"He obviously didn't want to say anything in
front of his friends. He told us this morning and
that's the important thing."

"I have to go back to my room before I meet
Annie. Are you going up?"

"I'm going to pick up a few things at the store.
Text me when you get the camera back, so we can
look at the file together."

She tossed her napkin onto her plate and rose
from the table, and Matt jumped up next to her.
"Be careful."

"You, too, and I hope you didn't put your trust

in the wrong person and Annie comes through for you."

"For us."

With a dry mouth, Matt watched Kylie stride through the lobby. He didn't like leaving her on her own, even in broad daylight.

He went up to his room and slid open the closet that contained the hotel safe. He punched in his code and grabbed the thick envelope already addressed to his attorney, Andy Tucker, in L.A. Some might call him stubborn, but he couldn't let this go. He wasn't going to end up like his old man.

Twenty minutes later he strolled into the post office, clutching the envelope. Only a few people waited in line, but Matt headed for the self-serve machine and scale. He didn't want anyone in this small town to know his business…not even Kylie.

He dropped the envelope onto the scale and touched the screen. As his fingers hovered near the dispenser to catch his postage, someone tapped him on the shoulder.

He jerked and spun around.

"Jumpy, aren't you?" Annie had her arms crossed over her chest and her fists bunched.

Matt pinched the postage between his fingers and pulled it from the machine. "That's what happens when someone sneaks up behind you."

She leaned forward on the scale with both hands

and left a small envelope on top of his. "What are you mailing?"

"Something personal. Everything go okay?"

"Perfect. Does that conclude my spying career?"

"That's it. Thanks, Annie. I owe you."

She held up her hands. "Let's not go there again. You owe me, and then I'll owe you, and then so on and so on."

"Let's just call it even then." He pulled her close for a quick hug. "And be careful with the chief."

"I'm going to be very careful with the chief." She winked and swept out the door.

Shaking his head, Matt swept the envelopes from the scale, dropped one in the repository for metered mail and folded the other one in half and shoved it in the pocket of his cargo shorts.

Time to find out what the C.C.P.D. wanted to hide.

KYLIE SLIPPED INTO the white, fluffy robe and pulled her hair out of the neckline. She wound it into a loose chignon. It had been a while since she'd had a massage, but she sure needed it. She had plenty of sore spots on her body from Matt's tackle yesterday, but without that tackle those lights would've knocked her out...or worse.

On bare feet, she padded into the short hall that led to the massage rooms and poked her head into number three.

"Hello?"

The masseuse wasn't here yet. Kylie stepped into the dimly lit room and inhaled the scent from the flickering lilac candle. There was another door in the room, and Kylie figured the masseuse would enter through that door.

Following the orders from the front desk of the spa, she slipped out of the robe. She hung it on the hook in the wall and lay facedown on the massage table, adjusting the sheet over her body. Then she positioned her forehead against the doughnut-shaped pillow and took a deep breath, closing her eyes.

The door clicked open, and Kylie said, "Hello."

The masseuse didn't answer, but Kylie heard rustling noises. A knock on the door caused her to flinch and must've surprised the masseuse, too, because she bumped into the massage table, jerking Kylie's head from its resting place on the pillow. So much for a relaxing massage.

A door opened and closed, and Kylie twisted her head around. The room was empty. Another knock on the door and a slightly accented female voice called out. "Are you ready, Ms. Grant?"

Kylie clutched the sheet to her chest and sat up. "Yes, come in."

A blonde, outfitted in a white jacket, glided into the room. "Oh, I didn't mean to startle you. I'm

Ingrid. Please lie down on your stomach and place your head against the pillow."

Kylie drew her brows together. "Another masseuse was in here before you."

"Really?" Ingrid turned to the sink to wash her hands. "Who was it?"

"I don't know. I was facedown and didn't look up."

"Probably someone forgot something in here. I'm sorry about that."

A layer of unease settled on Kylie's flesh. Why didn't the other masseuse say anything? Maybe she...or he wasn't supposed to be in here?

She rolled over onto her stomach and tried to get comfortable again.

Ingrid tugged the sheet from Kylie's shoulders to expose her back, and with firm hands coated with warm oil started on Kylie's neck.

"You have a lot of tension here."

Kylie sighed and closed her eyes again. *Ingrid, you have no idea.*

A LITTLE MORE THAN an hour later, feeling like jelly, Kylie slipped her key card into her hotel-room door. The connecting door to Matt's room stood open, and Kylie's breath hitched.

"Matt?"

"I'm here." His large frame appeared in the doorway. "Feeling better?"

Her thoughts flickered to the uninvited masseuse, but she snuffed them out. "Great. If you need a good massage, I highly recommend Ingrid. Did Annie come through?"

He held up the small camera. "Of course."

"I hope Chief Evans never finds out what she did."

"I think Annie has the chief under control. It wouldn't surprise me if she heads out with him when he takes his new job."

"It's that serious?"

"Annie is a woman on a mission."

"Some women just have to be with a man."

"Unlike other women."

Kylie ignored the leading question. "Did you have a chance to take a peek yet?"

"You asked me to wait for you, and I'm a man of my word." He jerked his thumb over his shoulder. "Besides, I knew you'd be tied up with the massage for a while, so I picked up some sandwiches for lunch. Is that okay?"

"That's more than okay. There's something about being totally relaxed that makes you starving."

"I have everything in my room if you're ready."

Kylie followed him into his hotel room and poured herself into a chair by the window.

Matt plunked a bag from the local deli onto the

table and began unwrapping sandwiches. "Turkey okay?"

"That's fine."

"Plain or barbecued?" He held up two bags of chips.

"I'll take the barbecued."

He fished two cans of diet soda out of the bag and plunked them down on the table. He tapped one can. "I saw a diet soda can in your trash."

"Very perceptive of you. I suppose it comes with the P.I. territory."

"I suppose." After pulling lunch out of the assorted bags, Matt sat on the love seat in front of the coffee table where his laptop sat and where he'd placed the camera.

"I'm going to start downloading the pictures, and we'll read the report straight from the laptop."

"Ah, modern technology."

"Makes spying a lot easier. Unfortunately, it makes crime a lot easier, too."

He took the second chair at the table and snapped open his can of soda. He touched it to hers and said, "Here's to more clues in the police report."

"Nobody saw you and Annie at the post office?"

He had taken a bite of his sandwich and circled his finger in the air while he chewed. He swallowed and wiped his mouth with a napkin. "Nobody that mattered. After his meeting with Mayor

Davis, the chief had a lunchtime meeting with the police chiefs in the neighboring coastal cities. No other cops around. Not that I think his force is all that loyal to Evans."

"This town never got over losing Chief Reese, and now it looks like his son, Dylan, is coming back to man the station."

"Dylan was a cop in San Jose."

"Oh, you kept in touch with him?"

Matt busied himself shoving an errant piece of lettuce back into his sandwich. "Yeah. Here and there. He played drums in a few of my bands in high school."

"I remember. You guys played at that one party at the Roarke brothers' house when their folks were out of town and the only reason the whole thing didn't get busted is because Dylan was the chief's son."

"Were you at that party?"

"One of the few I attended."

The laptop beeped, and Matt tossed his napkin onto the table. "I think it's done."

Kylie gulped her soda too fast and it fizzed in her nose. "In your face, Chief Evans."

Matt dropped to the love seat and Kylie settled next to him, her hip touching his.

He clicked a few keys on the laptop to complete the download and unplugged the camera from the computer.

"So how does this work?"

"Every picture is a page of the report. We can view it as a slideshow and just click through each page and read to our little hearts' content."

"What are we waiting for?" She reached across him and clicked on the first picture.

Side by side, they read through the preliminary information of the case. Some of the information they'd already seen from the redacted report Matt had obtained legally from the police.

When they got to the juicy part where the report started naming names, Matt flipped open his pad of paper and started taking notes.

"So Bree stayed with two girls while she was here. Mindy Lawrence and Patrice McNicoll. Do you know if they're still in town?"

"We can look them up in the phone book or maybe the guys from the other night know— Kenny, Rob and Toby."

"Okay, we'll check."

When they clicked to the next page of the report, they both gasped simultaneously.

Matt said, "You must've read what I just read."

"That Mindy reported Bree was friendly with Harlan Sloan?"

"Yep. What does that mean, *friendly?*"

"I guess we'll have to ask Mr. Sloan. What kind of friendly can a thirty-five-year-old man be with a nineteen-year-old woman?"

"Probably the very friendly kind, but Bree was nineteen—nothing illegal about that."

"Nothing illegal, but plenty immoral since Sloan is married, was married at the time."

"He wouldn't want her causing trouble, would he?"

"Nope."

They read through the rest of the page, where it was evident the police hadn't questioned Sloan very thoroughly, even though he'd had a text message on his phone asking Bree to meet him the night of her disappearance.

Kylie clicked her tongue. "I can't believe the cops let that slide so easily."

"Sloan claimed he had misplaced his phone and never sent the message. He also had an alibi at the time the message was sent."

Bree snorted. "Yeah, a couple of roadies who are dependent on him for their paychecks and their next gig."

At the end of the page, Kylie cinched Matt's wrist. "There it is. My mom's name."

Matt read the paragraph aloud, which stated on the day of the evening of Bree's disappearance, she had visited Rose Grant on Cressy Road.

"They questioned your mom, Kylie, and she had nothing to add."

"She wouldn't. She considered readings like a

therapist would consider a session with a patient—private and confidential."

Matt took her hand, palm up, as if doing his own reading of the lines that crisscrossed her skin. "Why did your mother commit suicide? She never left a note?"

At the sudden question, ready tears burned behind Kylie's eyes. "She didn't leave a note. I just always figured it was because she couldn't take the voices and sensations anymore. My mom was a tortured woman."

"You're not."

"We were different. My mom taught me what she was never able to do herself—filtering."

"Filtering?"

"I can turn things on and off. Mom was never able to do that. Can you imagine having flashes and feelings and voices assaulting you every time you met someone?"

"It could be useful in certain lines of work."

"It's hell. It's total confusion."

"And you don't get that? You don't shake someone's hand and immediately know, *I can trust this person,* or *This person is hiding something?*"

She leaned back against the cushion, but Matt kept possession of her hand, lightly encircling her wrist with his long fingers. "No. Sometimes I think my mom taught me too well. I have to be in the mood. It helps if I have an item belonging to the person. I have to concentrate."

"That's a good thing."

"I suppose."

"Your mom killed herself a few months after Bree's disappearance, right?"

"Yes, four."

"And the authorities were sure it was suicide?"

"I had the same thought when I went to Columbella House, Matt. I definitely felt a malevolent presence there, but the circumstances of my mom's death point to suicide."

"Okay, what if she knew something about Kylie's murder. What if she knew it was going to happen, did nothing to stop it and then couldn't live with herself?"

"That's what I thought when I had that dream the other night. In the dream, my mom was warning Bree." Or had she been warning her own daughter in affairs of the heart?

"Maybe she didn't voice her concerns to Bree. Maybe she wasn't specific enough and blamed herself for the girl's death."

"I don't know, Matt. It could be."

He hunched forward again. "Okay, let's get through the rest of this pathetic report. It's obvious why Chief Evans didn't want me to have it. This is a poor excuse for an investigation."

"I suppose you've seen a lot of police reports as a private investigator?"

He clicked through to the next page of the report. "Yeah, I've seen a lot of police reports."

They read about Bree's final interactions on the night she disappeared. Mindy and Patrice had reported that Bree had left them in the middle of the concert after receiving a text message, which they never saw, and which the cops later found out had come from Sloan's cell phone.

Matt tapped the screen. "She told them she was going to meet someone, but didn't give the name of the person. And that's it. She walked off the edge of the earth."

They clicked to the last page of the report that listed the people who had been interviewed.

Kylie's eyes skimmed through the familiar names, and then she froze.

"Matt, it's not just the ramshackle nature of the investigation Chief Evans was trying to hide from us." She poked at the screen.

Matt read aloud. "Eric Evans? Any relation to the chief?"

"Eric Evans is his son."

Chapter Ten

Matt swore under his breath. He should've known there had to be more to the chief's reluctance to hand over the full report. Then he thought about Annie.

"So the chief is married?"

"Divorced."

"Ex-wife and son still in town?"

"Ex definitely not. I don't think she ever lived here. The chief was already divorced when he took this job, divorced or separated."

"And the son?"

"Like most kids of divorced parents, he split his time between Mom and Dad, but he was already a teenager when his father took this job. I don't think he ever went to school here though—just summers and holidays."

"And is he here now?"

"I haven't seen him."

Matt's hands hovered over the laptop. "I don't get it. We didn't see an Eric Evans in the report, just his name listed at the end. What was his role in this tragedy?"

"I don't know. It must've been important enough for the chief to want to hide it."

Matt scrolled to the beginning of the report and did a search on Eric Evans. "It's coming up at the end only."

Kylie leaned forward, wedging her elbows on her knees and peering at the screen. "He must be one of those unnamed young people floating in and out of Bree's orbit while she was here."

She jumped back to the last page with the interviewees. "Look. Toby's, Rob's and Kenny's names are on here, too, but they don't appear in the report."

"Shoddy police work or an attempt to gloss over the fact that Eric Evans's involvement isn't chronicled in the body of the report?"

"Maybe a little of both, but I think we need to find Mindy and Patrice and start asking some serious questions."

"I think we need to ask Harlan Sloan a few serious questions, too, starting with that text."

Kylie slumped against the back of the love seat. "Wish I could ask my mom some serious questions, too."

"Looks like this report raised as many questions as it answered." Matt flicked the laptop with his index finger. "Let's finish lunch and get busy."

TWO HOURS LATER, Matt and Kylie stood at the hostess stand of the Whole Earth Café. Kylie nudged Matt in the ribs. "There she is."

Matt turned his head toward a waiflike young woman with wispy, light brown hair, juggling four plates laden with food. Coincidence that she worked in the same restaurant where someone had left a photo of Bree on their table?

Matt watched her buzz between two tables in the half-empty dining room, noticing an empty table for four between the two. He pointed at the table and asked the hostess. "Is it okay if we sit at that table?"

"Sure, go ahead." She waved them into the room.

As they slid into the booth, Mindy Lawrence glanced their way and her eyes widened. Matt whispered to Kylie. "Oh, yeah, we got the right girl."

Mindy crept toward their table, clutching a couple of menus to her chest. "Hello, welcome to the Whole Earth. My name is Mindy and I'll be your server."

"Hi, Mindy. When do you get a break?"

Her doe eyes got even bigger. "E-excuse me?"

Kylie shot him a look from beneath her lashes and put on a big smile. "Hi, Mindy. We're looking into the disappearance of Bree Harris, and we know she stayed with you when she was here for the concert. Can we ask you a few questions about that time?"

He had to learn not to be so abrupt in his questioning. He was a P.I. with no rights to this information, not a cop with every right.

Mindy's eyes darted to the right and to the left. "I guess so. As soon as these two tables finish up, I can take a break. Meet me at the benches behind the restaurant."

Matt smiled, too. "Thanks. We just ate, but you can bring us a couple of iced teas, and we'll wait for you."

When she scurried away, Kylie patted his hand. "That's better. You ever hear that expression 'You can catch more flies with honey than vinegar'?"

"I don't want to catch any flies, but I get your point."

A busboy instead of Mindy dropped off their drinks.

Kylie's eyes followed Mindy. "Why do you think she's so nervous?"

"Anyone would be nervous about questions regarding a disappearance and possible murder... especially if it involves the chief of police's son."

The people at one of Mindy's tables finished and left, and the people at the second table were paying their bill.

Matt left a few bills for the iced tea and a big tip, just so Mindy got the hint.

They left by the front door, and Matt steered Kylie around the corner of the building. An alley ran along the back of the building and across the alley, two benches faced a small street.

Kylie claimed the one awash in sunlight, and Matt stood in the shade next to it.

Ten minutes later Mindy rounded the corner, her elfin face sharp with worry.

Kylie patted the bench beside her. "Have a seat, Mindy."

The young woman perched on the end of the bench, looking ready for flight.

Matt shoved his hands in his pockets, determined to let Kylie handle the interrogation...or rather the questioning, or maybe just a conversation.

"Bree Harris stayed with you and your friend, Patrice, when she came to the festival, didn't she?"

"Yes. Patrice and I had met her when we all went to the Burning Man Festival in the desert."

"Burning Man?"

Matt cut in. "It's a concert with a bunch of indie bands out near Death Valley."

Mindy's pale brows jumped. "Yes, that's right. We'd met out there in the spring and we told her about Rockapalooza here at the Cove."

Kylie asked, "How long was she here before the concert started?"

"Almost two weeks. She was about to start her second year at UO—University of Oregon."

Matt cleared his throat. "She met a lot of people while she was out here?"

Mindy's gaze shifted to the side as she lifted a thin shoulder, her spaghetti strap slipping off. "Everyone meets a lot of people during the concert."

That small glance of Mindy's spoke volumes. Matt cleared his throat. "But Bree met a lot of people, didn't she? A lot of men."

Kylie's chin lifted, but Mindy nodded.

"Bree was really pretty. If you've seen her pictures, you know that. She attracted a lot of attention wherever she went and the guys really liked her."

"Did she have a lot of hookups when she was in Coral Cove?" Matt held up two fingers. "Not judging."

"Yeah."

Kylie blew out a breath. "Harlan Sloan? Eric Evans?"

"Those two definitely, but there were others. Bree partied hard and she had all the guys buzzing around her like flies."

Matt glanced at Kylie. Bree must've used a lot more sugar than vinegar.

Matt took off his sunglasses and wiped them on his T-shirt. "Again, not judging here, but did Bree do drugs?"

"She didn't use, but she definitely liked her booze."

Matt winced. "Could Bree have had an accident? Too much booze? Midnight swim in the ocean?"

Mindy's cheeks flushed. "She wasn't drunk that night."

"The last night of the concert?" Kylie hunched forward. "You and Patrice were the last to see her."

"She got a text and took off. That was it."

"Did you put that picture of Bree on our table yesterday with the note?" Matt kept the note of accusation out of his voice. After all, Mindy had been trying to help them with that message.

She lowered her lashes. "Yes. I'd heard that you were investigating the case."

Kylie put her hand on Mindy's arm. "Bree's body has never been found. Why do you think she's dead?"

Mindy lifted her head, her gaze darting from Matt to Kylie. "I just know she's dead. Sometimes you just get a sixth sense. You know what I mean?"

KYLIE STRETCHED OUT on her bed and flexed her toes. After questioning Mindy, she felt more like a P.I. than a psychic. She'd been on low ebb since that second night in Coral Cove when she fell from the balcony at Columbella. Since the night she'd run into Matt. She had no concentration. And she needed to get it back.

Matt grabbed on to the doorjamb of the adjoining door, and leaned into the room. "I suppose the Harrises didn't know their daughter got around so much."

"I didn't get the impression from Mrs. Harris that she knew, but that's not something a mother is going to blab about her daughter."

"She might want to if it would help solve the mystery of her disappearance."

"About that." Kylie crossed her arms behind her head. "I need to get my mojo back. I've been hanging out with you so long I'm beginning to rely on facts rather than feelings to investigate this case."

Without moving into the room, Matt crossed his arms, his large frame filling the doorway. "I thought you needed both. Isn't that how you've worked with police in the past?"

"I do need both, but investigative work is beginning to dominate the psychic connection I have with the victim." She swung her legs over the side of the bed, feeling vulnerable stretched out on the bed. "And I don't think I've ever worked so closely with a cop on a case…definitely no adjoining rooms."

"But I'm not a cop."

"Right, but I still need to get back to what I do best, or what I used to do best."

"How are you going to do that?"

"I'm going back to my mom's old house." She ran a hand through her hair. "I haven't been there since I got to Coral Cove."

"You're still looking for answers to your mother's suicide, aren't you?"

"Now I have an excuse. It looks like her suicide had something to do with Bree's disappearance."

"Bree didn't tell Mindy or Patrice what your mother said to her."

"No, but after Mindy made that comment about having a sixth sense, she did bring up Bree's visit to Mom. It must've made an impression on her."

Matt shrugged. "It's not every day people visit fortune-tellers, is it?"

"You'd be surprised."

"I know you don't like being joined at the hip with me—" Matt smacked the wall "—but I don't want to leave you on your own—not after that warning on your mirror and the incident with the lights…unless you want to go for another massage. At least you were safe there."

Remembering the uninvited masseuse, Kylie pursed her lips. Had it been safe?

"What's wrong? You didn't like the massage?"

Kylie bit her lip. The man had more heightened senses than she did right now. "The massage was great…."

"But what?" His sharp tone made Kylie sorry

she hadn't marshaled her automatic response to his comment about the massage.

She swept her hands across her face. "I thought my masseuse had come into the room, and then there was a knock on the door and my real masseuse came in and the mystery masseuse left through the other door."

Matt's jaw tightened. "Mystery masseuse? There was someone else in the room with you?"

"I was facedown. I didn't see the person. I just assumed it was my masseuse."

"What did your real masseuse have to say about it?"

"She said it could've been someone who'd left something in the room. She didn't seem worried about it."

"She didn't have a pair of klieg lights tipped over on her."

She put her hands on her hips to appear stronger than she felt because if she believed someone was stalking her, she'd never get her mojo back. "How would anyone else know I was having a massage?"

"I don't know, Kylie. How did someone break into your room? How did someone get up on that scaffold to dump those lights?"

"That could've been an accident." She threw her arms out to push away the idea that someone meant her harm.

"I don't like it." Matt squared his shoulders like

he really meant business. "For sure, you're not going out to your mom's old place by yourself. Does anyone even live there now?"

"Oh, God, no. After my mother's suicide, it turned into a mini Columbella. People think it's haunted out there."

"Who owns it?"

"Technically, my father—wherever he is."

"They held the title as joint tenants?"

"Yes, and when he took off, nothing changed. My parents never got divorced and never changed the title to the house. With the community property laws in California, my father legally owns the property."

"Who pays the mortgage and property taxes?"

"My father paid off the house years ago. He may still be paying the taxes, or they're in arrears." She brushed her hands together. "Not my concern."

"Except now the haunted house is vacant."

"Exactly."

"Which means you're not going out there by yourself."

"Don't you have to find out where Eric Evans is and have another chat with Harlan Sloan?"

"Why are you so anxious to get rid of me?" His lips twisted into a smile and the thought crossed Kylie's mind that no other woman in Matt's life had ever shot him down before. How could she explain to him that his presence scrambled her mind and destroyed her concentration? Other than that, she wanted to keep him as close as he'd allow.

"I'm not trying to lose you, but you need to keep on top of the other aspects of this case and let me worry about my mother's involvement."

"I'm a multitasker. Trust me."

Oh, she trusted Matt all right. It was herself she was worried about.

When they were making their way through the lobby, Matt poked her in the back. "Look, two o'clock."

"Huh?" Kylie swiveled her head around. What the heck was he talking about?

He bumped her shoulder and said, "Ahead, to your right."

She glanced to her right and picked out Harlan Sloan in the middle of a tight knot of people. "He's staying here?"

"Makes sense. It's the nicest hotel in town."

"I figured he might be staying at one of the hotels along the coast, even though this one's closer to the concert grounds."

Matt's breath touched her ear. "I think it's a good time to ask him a few questions, don't you?"

"Now?" Kylie choked. Matt had conducted a halfway decent questioning of Mindy earlier today, but interrogating Sloan in front of all those people didn't seem like a great idea to her.

"Maybe you should…" She was talking to thin air. Matt was already striding across the lobby.

She scurried after him and reached him just as he joined the group.

"Mr. Sloan? Matt Conner. We met yesterday at the concert venue."

Sloan raised his light blue eyes, which flicked to Kylie's face before returning to Matt's. "Ah, yes. We met and then there was the accident. Are you okay today, miss?"

"I'm fine, thanks." Kylie had slipped her hand in Matt's arm and was pinching the inside of his biceps.

"I'd like to ask you a few more questions, Sloan. We can meet in the bar later."

"You're a private investigator…not a police officer?"

"Yes." Matt's biceps tightened beneath Kylie's fingers.

"Since you're not a police officer, I'm not required to answer any of your questions, Conner." Sloan sealed his words with a thin smile stretching his lips.

"That's right, Sloan." Matt stuffed his hands in the pockets of his jeans and planted his motorcycle boots about a foot apart, right in front of Sloan. "But it's always better to get your story out in your own words, instead of someone else's."

The icy eyes seemed to pale. "I'll meet you in the lobby bar at five o'clock."

Matt grinned and his tough-guy persona melted in an instant. "See you then."

Kylie kept hold of Matt's arm as he strolled out of the hotel. When they hit the sidewalk, Kylie spun around. "Are you nuts? Why did you antagonize him?"

Matt lifted his brows. "He started it."

"You didn't have to get all large-and-in-charge and threaten him."

Matt widened his dark eyes. "Me? Threaten?"

"All that stuff about telling his own story."

"It's true. Most people would rather give you their version of events than have you depend on hearsay about them."

"Do you think he'll admit to an affair with Bree?" Kylie took the helmet Matt offered and pulled it onto her head.

"Probably, if he thinks we have a reliable source." Matt tucked some strands of her hair into the helmet and her face warmed beneath his touch. "But he'll put his own spin on it. That's the opportunity I'm offering him—his own spin."

"You're really good at this, aren't you? You must have some very satisfied clients."

"Let's just hope we can satisfy the Harrises." He straddled his bike and kicked up the kickstand.

Kylie climbed on the back, wrapping her arms

around Matt's waist for support. Beneath the cotton of his T-shirt, his abs felt like steel to her sensitive fingertips. The summer day was warm enough for T-shirts and no jackets, but Matt insisted she wear jeans on the bike...and his helmet. He went without, but no law enforcement in Coral Cove had pulled him over yet for not wearing a helmet, despite the law against it. And yet he wouldn't allow her to jaywalk.

He revved the engine of the bike and they took off with a jerk. She directed him off the Coast Highway inland, and pointed him down a one-lane dirt road that led to the home where she'd grown up and learned to harness her strange abilities.

The loud engine of the bike cut through the stillness of the trees. Nobody lived out here when Kylie had grown up and nobody lived out here now.

Matt cut the engine and planted his feet on the ground, walking the bike up the path to the house.

"It's isolated out here. How'd you get to school every day?"

"Shh, don't tell anyone, but I started driving my mom's beat-up car to high school when I was fourteen. Before that, I walked down to the school bus, which stopped at the foot of the hill."

"What is it you hope to discover here, Kylie?"

She pressed her fingertips to her temples where a dull ache had started as soon as the house came

into view. "I want to get in touch with my mom.
I want to get a sense of what she saw when Bree
came to see her."

"And you can do that here?"

"It's where her presence is the strongest. After
she killed herself, I was too afraid to come here.
Too afraid of what I might discover."

Matt tugged the helmet from her head and
brushed the hair from her forehead with one hand.
"What did you think you'd find?"

"My future. A future where I'd find it impos-
sible to live with myself. A future full of regrets
and mistakes."

Matt hung the helmet from the handlebar of his
bike and cupped her face with both of his rough-
ened hands. "Then don't live in a way that could
cause you regret later. Grab life with both hands.
Nobody can know the future, Kylie."

Her nose stung and her lower lip trembled. Was
he giving her an invitation?

He lowered his head and touched his lips to
hers. She wanted to kiss him back. She'd wanted
to kiss Matt Conner for a long time. And she didn't
want any regrets.

Standing on her tiptoes, she curled her arms
around his neck. And kissed him back with all
her might.

He swayed under her assault, and then stood
firm, cradling the back of her head with one hand

and tucking one arm around her waist. He dragged her close, sealing the length of his body against hers.

When he deepened the kiss, his tongue finding the warmth inside her mouth, he crushed her closer. Her toes left the ground and for a minute, she thought the sheer power of their connection had sent her airborne.

He murmured against her lips. "Mmm, you taste good, like sweet and spice and no regrets at all."

"And you taste like…heaven."

He grinned and settled her back on her feet. "Sweetheart, I'm the bad boy of Coral Cove, remember? I think you're confusing up and down."

"Can you blame me? Do you always sweep a girl off her feet when you kiss her?"

"I can't remember kissing any other girl."

She pushed at his solid chest. "You're very adept at the art of flirtation."

"I'm very adept at the art of truth." He blew out a warm breath that caressed her cheek and then landed a hard kiss on her mouth. "We need to talk when this case is over."

"If this case is ever over." She jerked her chin toward her mother's abandoned house. "We need some answers."

And how was that supposed to happen when she had the warm imprint of Matt's kisses on her lips?

The pounding in her head, which had receded

when Matt had taken her in his arms, returned full force when she turned her attention to the house. She took a step back, tripping over a rock on the side of what passed as a driveway.

Matt steadied her. "Do you have a way to get inside?"

She dug into the pocket of her jeans and curled her fingers around a key. She held it out, balanced on the palm of her hand. "I had this made at the time of Mom's death, but didn't have the courage to use it."

"Do you want me to wait out here?"

She didn't, but with Matt hovering nearby sending out those sexy vibes, she'd never get what she came for—communication with Mom.

"Please. If you don't mind."

"Do what you need to do. Just be careful."

Kylie took another step forward and hesitated. This house had always welcomed her in the past. When she'd graduated from high school and moved away, her visits back to this house when Mom was alive, although not always filled with happiness, had felt right and welcoming. Now some evil aura enveloped the house.

"What's wrong?"

Matt's voice made her jump.

"I'm not sure. Something feels off."

"Leave it, Kylie. Forget about your mother's involvement with Bree. The girl went to her to hear about her love life, and your mom delivered what she wanted to hear. Your mother had nothing to feel guilty about, but if she did—" he spread his hands "—there's nothing you can do about it now."

She looked at the house over her shoulder and shivered. She couldn't keep running away, no matter how unpleasant.

"I'm sure once I get inside, it will be fine."

She stalked toward the house, her sneakers crunching the dirt and gravel. Matt had drawn up next to her, his gaze searching the face of the house, the two windows in the front staring back at them blankly.

With the key held in front of her, Kylie walked up the two steps to the door and inserted the key.

It slipped in with ease and she cranked the door handle. She started to give the door a shove, with her foot against its base.

Matt bellowed behind her. "Back off, Kylie. Run!"

She whirled around, stumbling down the two steps. But she didn't have to run. A blast from inside the house propelled her forward and airborne.

Chapter Eleven

The heat from the blast penetrated Matt's skin as it tossed him backward through the air. Kylie's body tumbled past him and he stretched out his arms to cushion her landing. But she flew beyond his reach.

He hit the ground with a thump and immediately began scrabbling across the uneven ground to where Kylie's inert form had landed.

The blaze from the house crackled behind him and another explosion rocked the ground.

He reached Kylie and scooped her up in his arms. On his knees and clutching Kylie to his chest, he hobbled away from the blazing inferno.

When he'd reached a clearing several yards away from the house, he lay Kylie on the ground and bent over her, placing a hand on her chest. It rose and fell beneath his palm and he blew out a pent-up, acrid breath.

"Kylie, can you hear me?"

She moaned and her lids fluttered.

"Hang on. You're going to be okay."

At least her breathing sounded normal and she didn't have any burns that he could see, although the ends of her hair were singed.

He kept talking to her while he pulled his cell phone from the front pocket of his jeans. He punched in 911 and gave their location and the situation, even though he didn't understand the situation himself.

Kylie groaned again and opened her eyes. Her gaze wandered past his face and her limbs jerked and flailed.

"It's okay. You're safe now." He gathered her against his chest and stroked her hair, the crispy ends breaking off in his hand.

She coughed, bunching his T-shirt in her fists.

"Are you hurt anywhere? Are you burned?" The T-shirt covering her back had little holes in it, and he rolled the material up to inspect her skin. Red dots sprinkled her back, matching the holes in her shirt, but the rest of her flesh was smooth and unscathed.

"No." She croaked and cleared her throat. "My face."

He held her away from him and swept a swath of dark hair from the right side of her face. Angry red scratches and road rash marred her smooth cheek, and Matt's gut lurched.

"Looks like you landed face-first. You're going to be okay. How's your breathing?"

She sucked in a breath. "Okay. Wind knocked out of me."

Sirens wailed down the hill as black smoke continued to rise from the wreckage of the house. The emergency vehicles would have no trouble finding them.

Kylie touched her face and winced. "What happened, Matt? What did you see before I opened that door?"

"A wire." He pressed a kiss to her forehead. "Someone rigged the house to explode when the door opened."

Dr. Ames held out a tube of ointment to Matt. "This is for the little burns on her back. It will help them heal faster."

Kylie waved her hands. "Dr. Ames, I'm right here."

"I know, but you've had a shock."

"He had a shock, too." She wiggled her fingers toward Matt. "Look at his eyebrows."

Matt grabbed a hand mirror from the table next to the bed where Kylie was sitting. He waggled his singed brows up and down. "I could start a new trend."

The doctor tapped the side of Kylie's face with the tip of his gloved finger. "Don't bandage this.

Let it breathe. Reapply the antibiotic cream about three to four times a day and when it stops stinging, rub in a little vitamin E oil. There shouldn't be any scarring." He entered a few notes on his laptop and peered over the top at Matt. "And you're okay?"

"Flew through the air backward and landed on my rear end. Other than a sore tailbone and some unintentional eyebrow grooming, I'm fine."

"Then you're both free to go." He snapped the laptop closed and nodded at the nurse. "Are the police done questioning you?"

"I think so." Matt shot a glance at Kylie. "I'm not sure we're done questioning them."

"Did I hear right? A house was rigged to explode?"

"That's what it looks like."

"Crazy." The doctor shook his head. "Kylie didn't have any signs of a concussion, but keep your eye on her."

"I'll do that." Matt squeezed Kylie's knee.

When they got out to the hospital parking lot, Matt eyed his bike, which he'd ridden behind the ambulance to the hospital. "Are you sure you're okay to ride on the back?"

"I'm fine." She unhooked the helmet from the back. "You heard the doc—no sign of concussion, a few burns on my back, road rash on my face, and hair in desperate need of a trim, but other than that, I'm fine."

Matt climbed on the bike and held it still while Kylie slid on behind him. When she had her arms securely around his waist, he turned his head. "You knew, didn't you? You knew there was something wrong with the house before you walked up those steps."

"I sensed the evil, but I didn't know where it was coming from."

"It's coming from everywhere, Kylie. It's all around."

Thirty minutes later Matt fluffed up the pillows on Kylie's bed. "Lean back and relax. I put your cell phone, remote for the TV, water, burn ointment and ibuprofen on the bedside table. Did I forget anything?"

Kylie sank back against the pillows. "Just don't forget your civility when you talk to Harlan Sloan."

"If I see any hint from him that he had anything to do with the explosion, all bets are off."

"I don't get how Harlan Sloan would know anything about my mother or her house."

"Connect the dots. Sloan and Bree were friendly and Bree consulted your mom at her house. This is a small town, people know you, people know me."

Kylie squeezed her eyes closed. "Someone is desperate to stop this investigation."

"Is it enough to stop you?" Matt sat on the edge

of Kylie's bed, hoping it was. "I'm sure if you told Mrs. Harris the job was endangering your life, she'd understand. I'd understand."

"It's had the opposite effect." Kylie swept the tube of ointment from the nightstand and smoothed her finger along the outside of it. "The threats on my life mean Bree's killer is still here, and I'm going to find him. My mom couldn't help Bree, so I'm going to make up for that."

"And I'll be right by your side. Maybe we both have something to prove."

Tilting her head, Kylie parted her lips, but before she could ask any questions, Matt chucked her under the chin. "Don't open the door for anyone, not even the connecting door, which I locked. I have the key to your room, and I'll come straight back here when I'm done with Sloan. Call me if you need anything."

"Got it." She saluted him.

When Matt got to the door, he turned. "Hate to disturb you when you're all comfy, but come and put the chain on the door after I leave."

Kylie scooted off the bed and padded to the door where he was waiting. Matt laid a quick kiss on her mouth before stepping into the corridor and shutting the door. He waited until he heard the chain slide and then took off for his meeting with Harlan Sloan.

The elevator stopped on the way down, and

Kenny joined him, clutching a room service tray in his hands.

"Hey, man, we heard about the explosion on Cressy Road. That's messed up. Is your friend okay?"

"She's fine." Matt punched the button for the lobby. "How'd you hear about it?"

"Are you kidding?" Kenny's eyes bugged out of his sockets. "I thought you grew up here. Small-town people know what you ate for breakfast, they're going to know about a house exploding."

"You have a point." So everyone probably already knew that Kylie was Rose Grant's daughter and had the same psychic powers as her mother, and that she was here investigating Bree's disappearance. That's all anyone had to know.

"Kenny, do you know Eric Evans, the chief's son?"

"Yeah, I know him. He's back in town for the Rockapalooza."

And that's all Matt had to know. Thank God for small towns and small-town gossip.

When he walked into the lobby bar, he spotted Sloan at a small table, talking on his phone and making notes on a legal pad.

Matt pulled out the chair across from him, but Sloan didn't even look up.

The cocktail waitress delivered two beers to a

table in the other corner and then sashayed over to Matt. "Can I get you something?"

"I'll take a beer, anything on tap."

She tapped the rim of Sloan's empty martini glass and mouthed, "Another?"

Sloan nodded and then ended his call.

"Sorry about that, Conner. Business."

"And business is good?"

"I'm organizing two more music festivals in the next few months—taking advantage of the good weather while we still have it."

"Business wasn't so good for you after Bree Harris disappeared from the Coral Cove Music Festival."

Sloan leaned back in his chair and folded his arms. "That kind of tragedy always has a negative impact. The real businessmen behind these shows and the insurance carriers tend to be leery when a show garners bad publicity."

"You call a young woman's disappearance bad publicity?"

"And you call it opportunity." Sloan hunched over the table. "Cut to the chase, Conner. What have you heard about me and Bree Harris?"

"I heard you were friendly, and I heard she was obsessed."

The waitress set down their drinks and a bowl of some sort of mix of peanuts and pretzels.

Sloan plucked the toothpick lined with olives

out of his glass and slid the first one off with his teeth. "That's accurate."

"How friendly is friendly?"

"We had an affair. Is that what you want to hear?"

"Must've been brief. Bree was here for only a few weeks."

"It was." Sloan sipped his martini and closed his eyes. "Young women are always interested in men with power...I'm sure you've experienced that yourself, Conner."

Matt's pulse jumped. Looked like Sloan had done some investigating of his own.

"So you took advantage of your position?"

"I'm not going to lie. I always took advantage of my position. Young, beautiful women were always throwing themselves at me, and Bree Harris was no exception." He shrugged. "They used me, too. They wanted free tickets, backstage passes, introductions to the bands."

"But Bree wanted more."

"Foolish girl." For the first time since Matt had met the man, Sloan's face softened. "She fancied herself in love."

"She knew you were married?"

"I never lie to the women who come into my life. Can you say the same...Detective?"

Matt's fingers tightened around the handle of his beer mug. "We're here to discuss you, Sloan."

"Bree knew I was married, and I'd made it clear to her that I had no intention of changing my marital status."

"But she wouldn't leave it alone, wouldn't leave you alone."

"That's correct. I knew it would end when I left town and went on to my next gig. I didn't need to kill her to end the relationship."

"Unless she'd threatened to tell your wife."

Beads of sweat broke out on Sloan's high forehead and he mopped them with a cocktail napkin. "Bree was of legal age, but she was just a kid. She'd never make good on a threat like that."

"But she made the threat."

"Women say a lot of crazy things, Detective."

Matt clenched his jaw. "And your wife's claims of domestic violence?"

The cold eyes got colder. "Like I said, Detective, women say a lot of crazy things."

"What about that text from your cell phone to Bree?"

"Someone stole my phone to text her. Whether it was the killer or not, who knows? I had an alibi for that time and it satisfied the police."

Sloan downed the rest of his martini and slipped his phone in his pocket. "I've told you all I'm going to tell you. It's opening day tomorrow, and I have to get back to work."

Matt let him go without a fight. If Sloan had denied the affair, he would've looked guiltier. Sloan knew Matt had the goods on him, so of course he'd cop to the affair with Bree.

Sloan had the goods on him, too.

Matt dug into the peanut mix and popped a handful into his mouth. While he was chewing, Toby dropped into the vacant chair across from him.

"I saw you talking to Harlan Sloan. He's a slimy SOB."

"Is he still hooking up with the local girls?"

"Oh, yeah. It's not because he's a great guy or anything. They just want the perks he can give them."

Matt sipped his beer. Sounded like jealousy. "I saw Kenny in the elevator. He said Eric Evans is back in town. Do you know him?"

"Everyone knows Eric."

"He was acquainted with Bree, too?"

Toby's face sported two red spots. "I don't know about that. Eric's an okay dude. Did Kenny say that?"

"No." Matt pointed to a man in a black vest waving by the bar. "Is that your boss? I think he wants you back at work."

Toby grunted. "Can't have a few minutes' break. Heard about the explosion at Rosie Grant's old house. Hope your friend's okay."

"She's fine, thanks. I don't know why this town

insists on allowing these old houses to stand vacant. Same with that Columbella House. They should tag it and tear it down."

"No way." Toby's blue eyes kindled. "The house is a landmark for this town. How many coastal towns have a haunted house like that?"

"It's an eyesore." He smacked the table. "Looks like your boss is about to have a fit."

Toby glanced over his shoulder. "Well, I hope Kylie feels better. Sounds like she needs to be careful."

You have no idea.

THE KNOCK ON THE DOOR startled Kylie from her drowsy reverie in front of the TV. What did Matt say? He had the room key and he'd call her before he came up.

She slid her phone from the bedside table and checked for messages—none.

The door handle turned and the door yanked against the chain.

With her heart pounding, Kylie called out. "Who's there?"

The door slammed shut, and Kylie jumped from the bed. She laid her palms against the door. If she opened this door right now, she might come face-to-face with the person threatening her. But he might be waiting for her with a weapon.

She pressed her ear against the door. The chattering of maids slowed her heart rate a few more beats per minute. She gripped the handle of the door with a clammy hand and turned it. She poked her head into the hallway. A hotel maid was leaning on a cleaning cart, her head turned as she chattered with someone in Matt's room.

Kylie waved. "Hello."

"Hello. We're going into your room next. Do you want us to skip it and come back later? We're running really late already."

"Did you see someone in the hallway a few minutes ago?"

"No." She turned back to Matt's open doorway. "Maria, did you see someone in the hallway when we finished with the other room?"

Kylie held her breath. This could be it.

The maid in the hallway shook her head. "Sorry. She didn't see anyone either."

Kylie sagged against the doorjamb. "C-can someone get a master room key from your cart?"

The maid's eyes widened and her cheeks flushed. "No. Do you want us to clean your room now or later?"

"Later." Kylie slammed the door. The maid was lying. Someone had come along and lifted a master key card from the cart and had tried to enter Kylie's room while the maids were busy cleaning another room. And that person had done it before.

Her cell phone buzzed on the bed and she scooped it up. "I'm coming up. Are you okay?"

"Not really. I'll tell you when you get here."

Kylie perched on the end of the bed with bouncing knees until someone slipped a card into the door and once again it yanked against the chain.

"Kylie, it's Matt."

Relief flooded her body and she slipped from the bed. Peering through the crack in the door at Matt's tight face, she slipped the chain from the door, and he charged in.

"What happened?"

"Someone tried to enter my room, but the chain stopped him."

"With a key? He had a key card?"

"Did you see the maids' cart out there? I think that's where he got the key."

Matt slammed the wall with his fist. "How does that happen?"

"I think the maids were careless. The one acted very nervous when I asked her if there was a master key on the cart."

"How long ago was this?"

"Ten, maybe fifteen minutes."

"It couldn't have been Sloan. I was talking to him."

"Do you really think Sloan would do his own dirty work? Can you really see him skulking around my mom's house setting up an explosive trap? He knew I was alone while you were occupied with him in the bar."

"I don't know, Kylie." He kissed her cheek below the scratches. "Before we go out to eat, we're going to stop at the front desk and make a complaint about their lax security. We told them once already that someone had broken into your room to leave that message on the mirror."

"What did you find out from Sloan?"

"Not much. He admitted having an affair with Bree, and acknowledged that she'd taken it more seriously than he did."

"He'd have to admit to the affair because he had to know we already knew about it."

Matt snapped his fingers. "The local roadies, Kenny and Toby, both told me Eric Evans is back in town for the festival."

Kylie sucked in a breath. "Is he staying with his father?"

"I didn't ask, but if he is we're going to have to find him when he's not home."

"Do you really think Chief Evans is going to allow us to talk with his son?"

"He's a big boy. He's not going to be hanging on to his daddy's coattails the entire time he's here." He laid his hands lightly on her shoulders. "How are you feeling otherwise? Have you put any more ointment on your burns since your shower?"

"No. I dozed off in front of the TV after you left."

Matt patted the bed. "Lie down."

Kylie crawled onto the bed and flopped down on her stomach, hugging a pillow to her chest.

Matt tugged at the hem of her T-shirt. "May I?"

"Uh-huh." Kylie mumbled into the pillow to mask the rising excitement she felt at Matt's touch.

He rolled up her T-shirt, exposing her bare back to the cool air. She twitched when he dabbed the first bit of ointment on a burn on the small of her back.

"Did that hurt?"

"No."

He made his way up her back, skipping over her bra strap to get the burns on her upper back and shoulder blades.

"That should do it. They don't look too bad."

"They don't feel too bad, thanks to you." He pulled her shirt down and she turned and sat cross-legged on the bed. "If you hadn't spotted that trip wire on the door, I'd have been blown to bits walking into the house."

"I got suspicious when you started hedging. Turns out I trusted your instincts more than you did."

"How are the cops handling the investigation?"

"Checking for witnesses, checking out purchases of the items used to make the Molotov cocktail." He capped the ointment and tossed it onto the nightstand. "They may get lucky."

"They didn't get lucky with the investigation into Bree's disappearance, and I don't expect their luck to change until Dylan Reese replaces Evans as chief. We need to find Eric Evans."

"We can look for Eric Evans tomorrow. How about dinner and a movie in the room tonight?"

Kylie scooted off the bed, straightening out her T-shirt. "I know you're going to think I'm crazy... or crazier, but I need to go to Columbella House tonight."

"You're right...crazier. Why, after nearly getting yourself blown up, are you going to traipse around another abandoned house?"

"Nobody's going to booby-trap Columbella House. Anyone could walk into that house at any time."

"Which is exactly why you're not going there."

Kylie raised an eyebrow and flushed with warmth, not knowing whether to be annoyed by Matt's imperious attitude or flattered that he cared enough to forbid her to *traipse around.*

"I appreciate your concern, but someone blocked my first attempt at contacting Mom and he's not going to prevent me from my second."

"A trip wire connected to a Molotov cocktail is a little more than blocking you."

"I have to do it, Matt. I have to go to Columbella tonight." She glanced at him through the corner of her eye. "Of course, if you want to join me I won't say no."

He crossed his arms. "Wouldn't matter if you said no, *nyet* or *nein,* I'd be coming along anyway."

"After a quick dinner?"

"Pizza at Vinnie's and we take the car."

"It's a deal."

Later, they squeezed into Vinnie's at the height of the dinner rush and after a fifteen-minute wait, they grabbed a table in a corner beneath the big-screen TV blasting a baseball game.

They ordered a large pizza and a couple of sodas.

Kylie tapped his glass so the ice tinkled. "Are you sure you don't want a beer? I'm just having a soda because I don't want my senses dulled."

"I had my one drink for the day." He held up his index finger.

"You take your vow of teetotalism, or near teetotalism, very seriously, don't you?"

"You know what they say? Alcoholism is a disease, and it has a genetic component. I don't know why I just don't abstain completely—it's not like I'd miss it."

Kylie dropped another slice of pizza on her plate. "I wonder if I could've rejected my inheritance from my mother."

"It's not the same, is it? ESP isn't going to kill you."

"Really? Because I'm not feeling that way lately." She shot a glance across the room and gripped Matt's wrist. "Looks like this is our lucky day."

"You're kidding, right?"

She tipped her head toward a table of men commenting on the game in loud voices. "That's Eric Evans over there."

Matt turned in his chair to stare at the group. "Which one?"

"The guy with the Giants cap on backward."

"Time to introduce myself." Matt sucked down the rest of his drink and got up from the table.

Watching Matt stride over to the raucous table, Kylie covered her mouth with one hand. Matt approached every situation with both barrels blazing.

He leaned in toward Eric and gestured back toward their table. Eric nodded and pushed back from the table, and Matt returned alone.

"What happened?"

"Told him we had a few questions about his relationship with Bree Harris. Said he had to hit the john and he'd be right over."

"Must be your winning personality." She had no idea how Matt got all these people to agree to talk to him. Like Harlan Sloan pointed out, nobody really owed a P.I. anything. And they owed a psychic even less.

Eric ambled out of the restroom and pulled out a chair, straddling it. "Who's this?"

"This is Kylie Grant. She's my partner...for this case."

"Yeah, I know." Eric snapped his fingers. "You and your mom are gypsy fortune-tellers or something, right? Or your mom was until she offed herself."

Matt made a sharp movement and the liquid in the glasses sloshed from side to side. "Show some respect."

"Oh, hey, I didn't mean anything." Eric held up his hands. "I had a cousin who killed himself. Damned shame."

Kylie cleared her throat. "So what can you tell us about Bree Harris?"

"That girl got around."

"You mean she hooked up with a lot of guys?" Matt clenched his jaw into a hard line.

"She sure did." Eric outlined an hourglass in the air with his hands. "She was hot and she knew it. She'd been in town less than two weeks, I think, and had a lot of dudes sniffing after her."

Kylie wrinkled her nose at his crude expression. "And were you...sniffing after her?"

"I'm only human." Eric smacked the table and

shook his head. "That girl played everyone, and then I guess she got played in the end."

Matt asked, "So you had a relationship with her?"

Eric crossed one finger over the other. "Whoa. I didn't say that. I noticed her, I hit on her and she shot me down."

"Did that piss you off?"

When Eric's face twisted in anger, Kylie was glad Matt asked that question and not her.

"No."

"That's not what we heard." Matt scratched his chin and acted bored.

"Let me guess—you heard that from Mindy Lawrence."

Kylie swallowed. She didn't know much about questioning people, but she knew you didn't want to reveal your sources. "Why do you say that?"

"Because that chick was jealous of Bree. She couldn't hold a candle to Bree in the looks department, and she wanted a piece of that Harlan Sloan action for herself. I never got why the cops, my dad included, didn't look more closely at Mindy. She was the last one of her friends to see Bree alive, and the cops only had her say-so that Bree got some text and left the concert."

Great. Now they had everyone pointing fingers at each other. And Eric obviously didn't know that text had come from Sloan's phone.

"Eric, watch this replay." One of Eric's friends gestured to him from across the room.

"I gotta go." Eric jumped up from the table. "You'll never find out what happened to Bree if my dad couldn't." He strolled back to his friends and made a rude gesture at the TV.

Kylie sank her chin in her hands. "What do you think?"

"I think everyone connected to Bree is very free and easy about discussing how free and easy Bree was. Nobody denies knowing her, but everyone is quick to make the point that the girl got around."

"Do you think they're lying?"

Matt narrowed his eyes as he studied Eric's table of buddies. "I don't know. That means Mindy lied, too. And I don't feel like bringing it up with Mr. Harris. Their missing daughter's loose morals are not something you want to discuss with her parents."

"With Mindy, it could've been a matter of jealousy, like Eric said." Kylie crumpled her napkin and tossed it onto the pizza tin, littered with crusts. "I sure wish we could get in touch with Patrice."

"I've searched for her—last known address is Boston." He slipped the bill from the table and peered at it while reaching for his wallet.

"Oh, no you don't." Kylie snatched the bill from him and plunked down some ready cash. "I'm getting paid for this gig, too."

"You got it." He checked his watch. "Are you ready to go? I don't want to be creeping around Columbella at midnight."

"That just might be the best time."

Kylie drove out of town toward the coastline. When she stepped out of the car in front of Columbella House, she shivered—this time from the cool night air and not the hulking presence of the house. Tonight she felt ready, ready to reclaim the sensitivity that had been dulled by Matt's nearness… or rather replace the sensations that Matt's nearness inspired with the ones Mrs. Harris had employed her to use.

As they made their way to the side of the house and the patched-up kitchen window, Matt turned and said, "Someone may as well leave a key in the front lock. I don't get why that mayor isn't doing his level best to get Mia St. Regis back here to do something about this ruin."

"Since it was Tyler Davis's fiancée and Mia's sister who ran off with Mia's boyfriend, I don't think he wants to revisit the embarrassment."

"That was several years ago. Who cares about that anymore?"

She poked him in the back as he peeled back the plywood and reached through the gap to open the door. "Your father's reputation still bothers you. My mom's legacy still haunts me. Who are we to tell someone else to get over a trauma?"

"I suppose you're—" he clicked the dead bolt from the inside "—right."

Kylie made a move to open the door and he grabbed her arm. "Hang on. Do you remember what happened the last time you opened the door to an abandoned house?"

She stumbled back, square into Matt's chest, and he wrapped one arm around her waist and pulled her snug against his body while he ran his hand along the seam of the door. He let her go and crouched down to inspect the bottom of the door. "I think we're good."

Tucking her behind the broad expanse of his back, he blocked her entrance and swung open the door.

Kylie held her breath as if waiting for another explosion, but silence greeted their intrusion into the old Victorian and its secrets.

She scooped in a breath of damp sea air and shuffled into the kitchen behind Matt. A blast of sensations slammed her and she staggered back beneath their weight.

Matt craned his neck over his shoulder. "What is it?"

"I feel—" she pressed a hand against the base of her skull "—everything."

"Do you want to leave?" The light from the flashlight highlighted the furrows of worry stamped on his face.

"No." She pushed passed him into the entrance hall of the great house and tipped her head back to stare at the spot where her mother had hung herself.

Matt backed off and dropped into a stout armchair covered with some kind of white sheet. He set up the flashlight on a table next to the chair and steepled his fingers, watching her over the tips.

Kylie closed her eyes. Swirls of emotions battered her. Filter. Filter. She withdrew her mother's necklace and crunched the chain in her fist.

Mom, tell me what you know about Bree. Instead of an answer, three women cried out for help.

Three. Dead. Women.

MATT FOLDED HIS ARMS and clamped his hands against his body. Kylie had warned him on the drive over not to interfere. No matter what happened.

Watching her face contort and her body shake, he didn't know if he could follow those orders. She'd been through hell already today. He didn't want to see her go through any more…but it wasn't his call.

She took her gift seriously. She considered it her profession, just as he considered being a detective his. He had to respect that.

No matter what happened.

As Kylie's body went rigid and her lips moved

with silent words, a bead of sweat rolled down Matt's hairline. He let it travel to his jawline and drip off his chin, his own body as tense as Kylie's.

He swallowed against his tight throat, regretting the salty pizza he'd consumed hours ago—no, less than an hour ago. The back of his eyeballs burned and his muscles ached.

Five more minutes. He'd let her go five more minutes. Two more minutes. He shifted in the deep chair. He had to stop this.

As Matt coiled his muscles, Kylie let out a long breath. Her frame slumped, her shoulders rounding and her chin dropping to her chest. She looked ready to collapse to the floor.

Matt vaulted out of the chair and caught her as she began slipping. Her languid body felt boneless in his arms, and he swept her up and deposited her in the chair he'd just vacated.

"Kylie?" He cupped her smooth cheek—the one that hadn't been ravaged by road rash. "Come out of it, sweetheart."

Her long lashes flew open and her fingers, fashioned into talons, clawed at his shirt. A film clouded her green eyes, giving them the appearance of a misty sea.

"It's okay. It's Matt. I'm right here." He felt inadequate, more at ease rescuing her from an exploding house than trying to coax her out of a trance where she saw and heard things he couldn't fathom.

"Matt!" Her nails dug into his chest through the material of his T-shirt. "Matt, she's here."

He gathered both of her hands in one of his and kissed her stiff fingers. "Bree's here? In this house? What do you mean?"

Leaning forward, she shook her head, and her long hair with the crispy ends brushed his forearms. "I'm not sure. She's dead…and…and…"

She extricated her hands from his and pressed the heels of her hands against both temples. "Others are dead."

Matt's heart jumped. "What does that mean? Was Bree the victim of a serial killer?"

"No, no. At least I don't think so. Bree's dead and so is Marissa St. Regis."

"Marissa St. Regis? What does she have to do with this?" He massaged the back of her neck. "Calm down, Kylie. Take some deep breaths."

She panted and licked her lips. Her gaze, which had never fully focused on his face, traveled over his shoulder to the winding staircase. "We have to go upstairs, Matt. She's up there."

A chill touched his spine and he shook it off. "Bree's upstairs?"

Kylie rose from the chair and glided to the stairs. If she hadn't just been speaking to him somewhat coherently, he could've believed the trance still had her in its grip.

He followed her, trying to slough off the creepiness that had claimed his flesh.

She took the stairs, one step at a time, her footsteps creating a heavy and foreboding dirge.

Matt wanted to break the mood. He raised his voice. "What did you see, Kylie? Where are you going? What do you know about Marissa St. Regis?"

Ignoring every one of his questions, Kylie plodded on. She reached the second-story landing and turned her head toward the railing, blinking her eyes, as if expecting to see another body dangling there.

Then she continued across the landing toward the vast bedrooms. She stopped in front of one open door, cocking her head. "No."

"No, what? What are you looking for?"

She jerked her head toward the double doors at the end of the hall. That room must front the ocean side of the house, and it had to be bigger than the other rooms on this floor, given its heavy double doors.

Kylie seemed to hone in on this room and her pace picked up as she trod down the hallway.

Matt's heart hammered in his chest. Whatever force was drawing Kylie to that room couldn't be good. In a few long strides, he caught up with her.

"Let me go in there first."

She swiveled her head around, a surprised look in her glassy eyes, as if she'd forgotten his existence. She reached out a shaky hand and placed her palm against the closed door. "She's in there."

Matt doubted if the room contained Bree Harris but if Kylie sensed the significance of this room, he trusted her.

He nudged her aside. "Let me."

Grasping the handle of the door on the right-hand side, he pulled in a deep breath. He twisted the handle and shoved open the door.

A chilly breeze swirled through the room, tossing and twirling the drapes pulled aside at the open French doors, which faced the churning sea. The sound of the crashing waves reverberated in the room and Matt could almost feel the spray of salt water on his face.

Kylie crowded in behind him, her breath hot on his shoulder blade. "The doors are open."

Matt edged toward the French doors, his flashlight trailing over the four-poster, canopied bed and the wavy mirror that topped a claw-foot dresser. He stopped where the doors gave way to a wooden balcony and pointed his beam of light into the darkness of the night.

His heart lurched in his chest, and Kylie screamed in his ear as the light flickered over a body dangling from the top of the deck.

Chapter Twelve

Kylie clamped her mouth shut on the next scream that barreled up her chest. Her knees buckled, but Matt was there to catch her fall. Her rock.

He cursed and kicked the leg of an Adirondack chair to reposition it from its view of the body. "Sit."

He waltzed her three steps to the edge of the chair, since her muscles wouldn't obey any command she gave them to move, and settled her in its depths. She collapsed against the back of the chair, her head hitting the solid wood.

"Who is it?"

"Well, it's not Bree Harris."

The beam of light played over the figure, swaying grotesquely, pointed toes brushing the edge of the railing around the balcony. Light brown hair fluttered around a bent head, lifeless eyes staring into the crashing waves.

Matt approached the body, blocking Kylie's view of the all too familiar tragedy. He caught the woman's wrist between his fingers. Cursing again, he spun around and withdrew the phone from his pocket.

"It's Mindy."

Kylie drove her fist against her mouth. They'd just spoken to her that morning. Was it something they'd said?

"Matt…did we, I mean…"

"Shh." He crouched beside her and placed a steadying hand on her bouncing knee. "Don't start taking responsibility for this. Mindy was obviously a very disturbed young woman."

He barked into the phone, giving the 911 operator the location and situation. Then he took Kylie's hand. "We don't need to be in this spot."

As he led her off the balcony, she glanced over her shoulder. Another suicide at Columbella. "How long has she been there?"

"Not long."

By the time they reached the front of the house, they could hear the sirens coming up the road. An ambulance, a fire truck, and three cop cars came hurtling down Coral Cove Drive. The vehicles came to scattered stops along the street, and the emergency personnel poured onto the sidewalk and streamed through the front door, which Matt had left open.

One of the cops, Lt. Trammell, stayed outside

with Matt and Kylie. "The young woman hung herself?"

"It appears that way."

Matt had his arm around Kylie's shoulder—the only thing keeping her from slipping to the ground.

"Did you ID her?"

"Mindy Lawrence. Do you know her?"

Trammell's gaze darted up from his notepad. "That young waitress at the Whole Earth?"

"That's the one."

The lieutenant sighed. "She had a drug problem."

"She did?" Kylie's voice squeaked. Maybe Mindy's suicide had nothing to do with their questions about Bree and the memories of her disappearance—of course, that didn't make Mindy's suicide any more acceptable.

"We'd picked her up a few times for possession." He tapped his pencil. "How'd you two happen to be here?"

Matt hugged her closer. "Kylie's mom killed herself here, too. She was just trying to get some closure."

"Yeah, I remember that. Sorry." He pushed the hat back on his head. "Damned creepy coincidence, but then I never liked this house. Just this summer, we had a couple of incidents and a few more people died here. When's it going to stop?"

Matt said, "Maybe when Mia St. Regis tears this place down."

Lieutenant Trammell questioned them for another fifteen minutes before heading into the house. "You two don't have any plans to leave town, do you?"

They shook their heads and walked out to the car parked amid the flashing lights. Kylie squinted at the vehicles. "When are they going to take her out of there?"

"When the coroner's van shows up."

She grabbed the handle of her car door. "Do you think it had something to do with her drug use?"

"I don't know." He leaned against the car. "Do you think it had something to do with our investigation?"

"What if—" she bit her lip and stared at the house "—what if her death wasn't a suicide?"

Matt ran a hand through his short hair. "Here we go again. It pretty much looked like a suicide to me."

"What if someone lured her here? Knocked her unconscious and then strung her up to make it look like a suicide?"

Matt opened the door for her and nudged her inside the car. "Then the autopsy will show that. But why would someone want to kill Mindy now? We already talked to her. She told us everything she knew."

"Did she?"

Matt slammed her door and stalked to the other side. "And if she didn't tell us everything, how would the killer know one way or the other what she said?"

Kylie gripped the steering wheel and rested her forehead between her hands. "My mom knew Bree was in trouble, Matt. That's why she killed herself. She knew and she didn't warn her."

"Is that what you got—" he jerked his thumb at Columbella House "—from there?"

"I could feel her regret."

"Would she have known the specific threat against Bree? The specific person?"

"No. Just that she was in danger."

"She probably did warn her, Kylie. She warned her and Bree wouldn't listen."

"Maybe, but she wasn't able to prevent Bree's murder."

"Maybe you and your mother didn't receive your gift to prevent. Fate may have already been in play."

She turned her head and studied his face. "You believe in fate like that?"

"Who knows?" He brushed a strand of hair from her battered cheek. "Fate brought me here to work with you, even to save you a few times."

Her lashes fluttered at his sweet touch. Then she blinked as headlights flooded the car, and she peered into the rearview mirror. "I think that's the coroner's van."

"Let's get out of here. It's been a long day."

She turned on the engine, and Matt touched her arm. "What did you mean back there about three dead women?"

Kylie eased the car forward and made a U-turn while taking a last look at Columbella out the window. "Mindy, Bree and...Marissa St. Regis. She's dead, too."

THE HOTEL BUZZED with life and activity. Kylie took a deep breath and soaked it all in. Life, not death. She didn't even mind when a couple of preteens left puddles of water in the elevator after their dip in the hotel pool.

When the doors closed on the kids' giggles, Matt raised his brows. "Looks like everyone is having a late night. It's close to eleven o'clock."

"History repeats itself, doesn't it?" Kylie slumped against the elevator wall.

"Listen." Matt grabbed her shoulders and pinned her against the wall, straightening her posture in the process. "You had no idea Mindy was going to kill herself. You weren't questioning her as a psychic. You were questioning her as a detective, and detectives don't know that stuff. So don't get any crazy ideas about blaming yourself for her death."

She tilted back her head. "I was not blaming

myself for Mindy's suicide. Don't worry. I'm no more like my mom than you are like your dad."

His grip loosened into a caress, and he traced a thumb along her throat. "Good to hear. So when you said history repeats itself, you meant Mindy and your mom, not you and your mom."

"That's right." She couldn't help the silly smile that claimed her lips. "But thanks for your concern."

His dark eyes got darker as they dropped to her mouth, but the elevator doors slipped open on their floor before he could make good on their promise.

Her shoulder bumped his arm as they walked down the hotel corridor in silence. She stopped at her room, and Matt crowded her as she unlocked the door, giving every impression that he intended to follow her inside.

And she had no intention of stopping him.

When they entered the room, Matt took a turn around it, even poking his head into the bathroom and whipping aside the shower curtain.

"All clear?" She bounced on the end of the bed and flicked on the TV.

He held up his index finger and left her room, pulling the door closed behind him. She could hear him going into his own room next door, and several seconds later he slid the lock on the adjoining door and knocked.

She pulled it open and he jerked his head back toward his room. "Now it's all clear."

Leaving the connecting door open, Matt sauntered to her mini fridge. "Is this your own water or the hotel's?"

"That's mine. Help yourself."

He took two glasses from the credenza and poured water into both. Handing one to her, he said, "You probably need something stronger. We can go back down to the bar if you want."

"Water's fine." She held out her hand and he gave her the glass.

He sat in a chair and stared at the talking heads on the TV. "So you knew Mindy was dead and Marissa St. Regis and we already figured Bree was dead, but were you able to see how or why?"

Kylie gulped some water and put a hand to her head. "It was all too confusing. You'd think Columbella House would be a great place for a medium to communicate with the dead, but there's so much death in that house it all becomes one big jumble."

"Like information overload?"

"Something like that. All those women were clamoring to send me signals, anything important got lost in the maelstrom." She pinned her hands between her knees. "That's how it was for my mom almost all the time. She had no filters."

"She had no filters when it came to you either,

did she?" He sat next to her on the bed, and the mattress dipped so that she tilted toward him. "She warned you about everything and everybody."

Her gaze flitted to his strong jaw and the sympathy in his dark eyes. "Yes."

"Terrible burden to place on a child, on a young woman."

"She was just trying to protect me."

"But she regretted placing that load on your shoulders."

"How do you know that?"

"Because in the end, she didn't want to do the same thing to Bree. She sensed some danger, but she let it go that time. Bree had probably come to her full of excitement and high hopes for the future, and Rosie didn't want to dash those hopes... like she'd dashed yours so many times."

Her nose stung and she blinked her eyes against the tears that threatened to spill onto her cheeks. How many times had her mother warned her against boys, dating, getting into a relationship? Just because her own had failed, she didn't want her daughter to suffer the same fate.

But Mom had chosen a man who couldn't handle her gift...and Kylie hadn't blamed him. Even sharing Mom's gift, Kylie'd had a hard time living with her. In the end, that's why she moved away.

But Matt wasn't like her father. Matt admired her gift, respected it.

He tucked a lock of hair behind her ear, his finger tracing her lobe. "I've brought back some sad memories."

A smile trembled on her lips. "You brought me a lot more than that, Matt Conner."

Cupping her face with one hand, he brushed his lips against hers. Then he kissed her again, this time sealing his mouth over her mouth. The tentative touch became hard and demanding. And she answered the call.

He moved closer to her on the bed, and she sank against him, brushing her breast against his chest. He draped an arm around her shoulders and fell back on the bed, taking her with him. They turned toward each other, their legs still dangling over the side of the bed, tangling and twining.

He pulled his T-shirt over his head and Kylie gulped at the shifting slabs of hard muscle displayed on his bare chest. She ran her palms over his smooth flesh, sprinkled with springy black hair, and he sucked in a breath.

Her hands trailed down his flat stomach, and he cinched her wrist with one hand. With the other, he bunched the material of her T-shirt in the front.

"May I?"

She glanced at his fist. "You're not going to rip it off me, are you?"

"Sorry." He released her T-shirt and smoothed

it across her belly. Then he rolled it up, and she lifted her arms so he could pull it off.

After he shoved the T-shirt to the floor, he slipped one warm hand under her back and unclasped her bra. He skimmed his hand to her front and cupped one of her breasts.

He nudged her bra aside with his nose and kissed the tip of her nipple, sending a river of shivers down to her toes. He gathered both of her breasts and buried his head between them. "Mmm, I love your curves. I want a woman who's not going to break."

Straddling her, he rose on his knees and tugged at the button on her jeans. He yanked them, along with her panties, over her hips and tossed them both over his shoulder.

As his gaze raked her body, she squirmed, feeling, well…naked. And exposed. She felt exposed.

She hitched her arms around his waist, pulling him down. His long, large frame flatted against her, whooshing the air from her lungs.

Hiking up on his elbows, he grinned. "Sorry about that—almost knocked the wind out of you."

"You take my breath away, anyway." Her hands clawed at his belt and fly. When his jeans gaped open in the front, she shimmied her hands down the back and dug her fingers into his muscular buttocks.

He groaned and sat up again. "It's a lot easier to get undressed *before* we get into bed."

Rolling to the side, he yanked his jeans off and kicked them to the floor where they joined hers.

She drank in his naked body and reached out for him. When he made a move to lie next to her, she stilled him with a flat hand on his belly. "Wait."

Her hand trailed to his erection, and she caressed his smooth, tight flesh. Matt squeezed his eyes closed and hissed through his teeth. When she closed her lips around him, he dragged his fingers through her hair.

His voice rasped from his throat. "You're going to drive me crazy."

She wanted to drive him crazy. She wanted him to desire her without pity or a comforting hand. She didn't need slow and tender and sweet.

He withdrew from her mouth and nudged her back against the pillows. Then he straddled her again and outlined the curves of her body with his rough palms.

"You're a goddess."

He entered her at the same time he landed a hard kiss on her mouth. Nothing slow, tender or sweet about him now. His tongue invaded her mouth, keeping pace as he drove into her, hard and fast.

She met every thrust, curling her legs around his strong frame, holding on for dear life.

He slipped a hand between their bodies and

molded her breast. He broke away from their heated kiss and sucked her nipple into his mouth. A zap of pleasure shot down from where his mouth was sealed over her flesh to where their bodies were sealed together.

The tingles spread to her toes, and her muscles tightened as she clamped her legs around him tighter. Talk about someone who wasn't going to break. Matt's body was solid…hard.

Just as Matt finished with the first breast and turned his attention to the second, Kylie felt the heat and pressure build in her belly. He licked her nipple…just once…and the tension in her body unraveled.

Pleasure suffused her in warm, liquid waves. Her legs fell from around his waist. She flung her arms over her head, which lolled to the side.

Matt chuckled and kissed the side of her neck. "I think that worked better than the massage."

She blinked and widened her eyes. "Are you… have you…"

"Me? I'm just getting started."

After using his tongue, his mouth and his hands to reduce her further to boneless ecstasy, he encircled her ankles with his fingers and tugged her legs over his shoulders. He loomed above her, his face dark with desire and primal need.

He filled her again and again until he shuddered once, lifting her bottom from the bed. He looked deep into her eyes as he climaxed, bringing her along for the ride.

He collapsed beside her and traced a bead of sweat between her breasts with his tongue. "You are a feast of sensual pleasures."

"How poetic." She lifted an eyebrow in his direction. "And did you get your fill?"

"Not—" he kissed her ear "—quite."

His words and the way he worshipped every inch of her body flooded her with a deep satisfaction. She'd fulfilled him on every level in every way. It wasn't one-sided.

He pulled her close, his warm, damp skin reawakening every cell in her body. When he stroked her back, she arched against him.

She kissed the hollow of his throat where his pulse beat against her lips, a slow, steady beat.

"Kylie…"

Whatever he was about to say got cut off by someone pounding on the door of his room.

Matt's hand froze on her back. "Who the hell could that be at this hour?"

They soon had their answer.

"Conner! Conner! Open this door. It's Chief Evans and we gotta talk."

Kylie tipped back her head to look into Matt's face. "Is he kidding?"

"Does it sound like he's kidding?" Matt rolled from the bed and snagged his jeans from the floor.

He stuffed one leg inside and hopped to the closet where he yanked a terry-cloth robe from a hanger. "You'd better put this on if you want to hear what he has to say."

Rolling her eyes, she shoved her arms into the sleeves. "It would be kind of hard *not* to hear what he has to say."

He glanced over his shoulder. "Are you decent?"

She tied the sash of the robe and nodded.

Matt peered through the peephole, detached the chain and threw open the door. "What is it, Chief? You're going to wake up the whole floor."

Chief Evans stormed past him and stopped when he saw Kylie, his eyes narrowing. "Good. You're both here."

"Kylie has the room next door, after the attempts on her life..." He trailed off as Evans's gaze darted from Matt's bare chest to her robe. "What do you want?"

The chief leveled a finger at Matt. "I want you to stop harassing my son."

Matt's lids dropped half-mast over his eyes as he stared at the accusatory finger. The chief licked his lips and dropped his hand.

"Harassing? Is that what he told you? We just had a few questions for him."

"Why?"

"He knew Bree Harris. He was around at the time of her disappearance."

"How do you know that?"

Matt shrugged. "Common knowledge."

"Then it should also be common knowledge that Eric didn't have anything to do with that girl's murder."

Kylie shoved her hands into the pockets of the robe. "Oh, now you're calling it murder? You'd always treated the case as a missing person."

"I'm not naive, Ms. Grant. Just because we never found the body, a murder weapon or had a suspect, we never doubted Bree had been murdered."

"Seems like there were plenty of suspects."

"But not my son." He smacked his fist into his palm. "Lay off."

Matt wedged his shoulder against the wall. "We'll go wherever this investigation takes us, Chief."

Evans stopped at the door and turned. "You do that and I'll have your brand-new P.I. license. Private investigator. What a bunch of bull. You lost your job with the LAPD for being a screwup, just like your old man. What makes you think you can do any better as a P.I.?"

He slammed the door behind him, but Kylie didn't even flinch. She met Matt's eyes and saw the truth. Finally.

He'd been lying to her all along.

Chapter Thirteen

Matt made a move toward her, but she held out a hand. He could overcome all her doubts and fears just by holding her, and she didn't want that...not now.

The chief's parting words had socked her in the gut, and she folded her arms across her stomach. No wonder Matt had never answered any of her questions about his previous cases. He didn't have any previous cases. This was his first.

Had he been lying about the drinking, too? Evans had accused Matt of screwing up like his father. Was he an alcoholic? Had he been using her this whole time to make a good impression for his first case?

"Kylie." Deep lines marred his face, and he hadn't dropped his hand.

"You lied to me."

"I didn't lie to you."

"You misrepresented yourself."

"I'm a P.I. working on the Harris case. Mr. Harris hired me. That's not misrepresentation."

"It's not the whole truth either." She swallowed and yanked on the sash of the robe. "Why didn't you tell me you'd been a cop? Why didn't you tell me about your...your screwup?"

"I was going to tell you. I'd planned to tell you after we solved this case."

She snorted, trying hard not to cry. "After *we* solved this case? You mean after you used my talents to solve it, so you could run back to Mr. Harris with your first triumph."

Two red spots formed high on his cheekbones and his dark eyes flashed. "Is that what you think?"

"What am I supposed to think? If you're not upfront with me, it leaves me to form my own conclusions. And that's the one I formed."

"You're wrong." He finally dropped his hand, shoving it into his pocket. "I want to explain everything to you."

"Oh, now you want to explain everything—now that Chief Evans has blown your cover."

He laughed, a dry sound that contained no humor. "It's not a cover, Kylie. Something...unpleasant happened to me at the LAPD and I didn't want to burden you with my problems. Not in the middle of this case. Not when you had your own issues."

"How thoughtful of you."

He shrugged. "Do you want to hear the story now?"

"In bed so you can sweet-talk me?"

His eyebrows jumped to his hairline. "The last thing I want to do with you in bed is talk."

Her belly fluttered and tingles raced across her skin. She turned so he couldn't see her confusion. She wanted to be mad at him for keeping an important part of his life from her, a part that could impact their investigation. But the man had saved her life—twice. He'd been there for her.

It couldn't have all been an act.

She glanced over her shoulder. "You know, Matt, I don't want to hear it right now."

She stumbled through the door connecting their rooms and slammed it. Then she locked it.

Crossing to the foot of the bed, she took in the jumbled covers and Matt's boxers and T-shirt crumpled on the floor. She fell face-first onto the covers and inhaled Matt's musky, masculine scent.

I told you so. You can't trust men.

Kylie grabbed a pillow and covered her head. "Not now, Mom."

MATT FELT THE SLAM of the door like a slap to the face. He slumped in a chair by the window, propping his bare feet on the windowsill.

He figured she'd find out about his dismissal

from the LAPD before he had a chance to tell her. He hadn't meant to hide it from her.

Or had he?

The termination hadn't been his fault but he'd had a hard time convincing anyone of that except his partner and his attorney. Hell, maybe Andy didn't even believe him.

He didn't want Kylie to see failure when she looked at him. He'd been her hero the past few days. He always had to be the hero, always had to be the knight in shining armor. It gave him his sense of worth.

How pathetic was that?

He kicked against the windowsill. He should've told her from the beginning. She'd probably always carried warnings in her head from her mom about guys like him.

But she'd been having second thoughts about her mom's advice since Rosie's suicide.

He'd met Kylie at precisely the right time—when she'd decided to can Rosie's dire warnings and trust her own instincts. Like a ripe peach, she'd fallen into his lap, and he'd been ready with his superhero act to take a big, juicy bite.

After Evans blurted out the truth about his past, Matt had crashed back into the phone booth. And he'd have to pick up the pieces.

Not just for Kylie, but for himself.

He pushed up from the chair and stripped off

his jeans. Yanking the covers back on the bed, he glanced at the solid door between his room and Kylie's. She had his boxers and his T-shirt.

Naked, he slid between the smooth sheets. That's not all she had…she had his heart, too.

The following morning, Matt rubbed his eyes against the sun spilling through the slit in the drapes. He fumbled for the hotel alarm clock on the nightstand and held it two inches from his face.

He dropped the clock on the bed. The superhero had overslept. Must've been all that rescuing yesterday…and the good sex.

He slid out of the bed, dragging half the coverlet with him, and then dug through his gaping suitcase for a pair of clean boxers.

Grimacing at the closed adjoining door, he walked up to it and tapped. "Are you awake?"

Silence.

He tried the door handle, but she'd locked it after she slammed it in his face. He knocked louder. "Kylie? You in there?"

The continued silence caused his heart to hammer. Kylie didn't get up as early as he did, so maybe she was still sleeping. Maybe the good sex had worn her out, too.

He grabbed the receiver of the hotel telephone and punched in her room number. The phone rang in stereo—in his ear and in Kylie's room. With each unanswered ring, his heart rate hitched up another two beats. He slammed the receiver in the cradle.

If she were sleeping, the ringing phone would have awakened her...unless she knew he was on the other end and she wanted to torture him.

With tension tightening knots in his gut, he stepped into the boxers and scooped up the jeans he'd been wearing last night. He pulled on a T-shirt and shuffled into a pair of flip-flops and rocketed out of his room.

He paused at Kylie's door in the hallway and banged his fist on it. "Kylie, are you there? I'm about to go ballistic in thirty seconds, so don't mess with me."

He pressed his face to the paneled door and heard his own heartbeat reverberating in his ear.

A housekeeping cart trundled down the hall and Matt sprinted toward it, startling the maid behind it. "Can you open room three twenty-six for me?"

The hotel maid's eyes widened. "No. A lot of trouble on this floor. I don't open doors for nobody."

"Okay, okay." Matt held up his hands and backed away from the cart toward the elevator. He smacked the button and then jogged for the stairwell.

In the lobby, he scanned the tables in the café. He descended one more floor and poked his head inside the gym and the pool area. A few kids stopped screaming and splashing long enough to eye him with distrust. Guess they knew he'd lied about getting canned from the LAPD, too.

He paced in front of the reception desk while the two clerks handled other guests. When one was finally free, Matt lunged forward and hunched over the counter.

"You know the woman I've been with...I mean, my friend? Long, dark hair, about medium height?" Matt held his hand shoulder high.

"Sure, I know her. Ms. Grant."

"Yeah, that's right. Have you seen her this morning?"

The hotel clerk raised his brows and glanced over his shoulder.

Matt flattened his palms on the counter. "You know, she was near that house that got blown up yesterday. We have adjoining rooms and I didn't hear her get up this morning. I'm concerned about her."

The muscles in the man's face relaxed. "Yeah, I heard about the explosion. Ms. Grant left this morning, over an hour ago."

Matt swallowed. Why would she go out alone when she had a target on her back?

"I suppose you don't know where she went?"

"Couldn't tell you that, but she'll be okay."

"Really?" What did this pipsqueak know about the dangers stalking Kylie?

He waved his hand. "She left with Kenny and Toby. They work here, and I've seen her talking to them before."

Matt blew out a breath. Did those guys have more information for her? Another clue?

Did they understand that someone had Kylie in his crosshairs?

"By the way, Mr. Conner. A package, a box, arrived for you yesterday. You had to sign for it, so we sent it back to the post office." He slid a slip of paper across the counter. "Here's the receipt to pick it up."

"Thanks." Matt frowned at the post office receipt—a package from L.A. Must be from Andy and he'd started sending stuff to the hotel already.

A commotion at the hotel entrance made Matt jerk up his head. Harlan Sloan breezed into the lobby with his usual entourage of groupies and yes-men. His gaze flicked toward Matt and then trailed back again. He dropped his shoulders as if coming to a decision and approached Matt.

"I heard about that young woman who hung herself last night."

"One of the last people who saw Bree Harris alive."

"Guilt is a terrible emotion to bear."

"You speak from experience?"

"I think we all have our regrets, Detective."

"I was set up."

A light kindled in Sloan's cold eyes. "I had an ownership interest in the club you raided that night."

Matt nodded. The news didn't surprise him. Sloan had him pegged as a cop from the get-go. "Then you were set up, too, because that drug dealer and his stash of money and drugs were planted."

"Clubs come and clubs go." Sloan smoothed back a lock of silver hair. "It didn't ruin *my* life."

"Didn't ruin mine either. Have you seen Ms. Grant?"

Sloan clicked his tongue. "You misplaced the medium?"

"She's not my possession."

"Could've fooled me." He turned and then stopped short. "Any luck finding out what happened to that poor girl?"

"We have a few leads." *Like the killer is still in town.*

"That's good. That's good." Spinning around, he clapped his hands at his minions. "It's a go, people. First sound check in less than an hour."

Matt ran his tongue around the inside of his dry mouth. The music festival started tonight. Were he and Kylie really any closer to finding out the truth?

He glanced up when the front doors of the hotel swooshed open and warm relief soaked into his skin as Kylie floated into the lobby, distraction clouding her eyes. He strode up to her, not knowing whether to kiss her or shake her.

"Where were you?"

"I ran into Kenny and Toby at breakfast this morning, and they told me another roadie remembered seeing Bree the night she disappeared."

"And you just ran off with them without telling me?"

Her lips flattened into a stubborn line. "You're not my bodyguard, Matt. In fact, maybe we should go our separate ways on this case."

On this case or in their lives?

"You're not going to allow that misunderstanding between us to endanger your life, are you?"

"It's broad daylight. I took a couple of waiters over to the concert grounds and interviewed a roadie."

"It was broad daylight when the lights almost crashed on your head and when you stepped into a house rigged for explosives."

"Right." She fashioned her fingers into a gun and shot at him. "And you were there both times and couldn't stop those events from happening."

"No, but I…" He pinched the bridge of his nose. He wasn't going to remind her that he'd saved her from something worse on both occasions. "What did you find out? Why didn't this guy say something before?"

"He's with one of the opening bands and arrived

last night. This band played three years ago, too, and Charlie, that's the roadie's name, remembered Bree from when he was here before."

"Did the police ever question him? I don't recall his name in the report."

"He got sick, left early and didn't even realize she'd gone missing until some people were talking about it last night."

"What did he say?" Crossing his arms, Matt watched the play of emotions across Kylie's face. She really was considering holding out on him.

She puffed out a breath of air between tight lips. "He saw her backstage that night, so I guess Sloan did get her backstage passes even though he was dumping her. She was tipsy, stumbling around a bit."

"Ripe for someone to take advantage of her."

"That's what I thought."

"You looked—" he pinched her chin between his thumb and forefinger "—disturbed when you walked in here."

"Did I?" Her cheeks turned pink at his touch.

So he wasn't the only one who still felt that electric current flowing between them.

"Did something happen out there?"

She shook her head, dislodging his fingers. "No. It's just…"

"Yeah?"

"Creepy."

"The concert?"

"I have this feeling that something is going to happen again." She pressed her hands to her cheeks and sank onto the edge of an ottoman strategically placed in the lobby.

"A *feeling* feeling? Or just a feeling like the rest of us mortals?"

She didn't even crack a smile at his lame attempt at a joke. Must be a *feeling* feeling.

"It's in the air, isn't it? It's hot today. Hotter than usual for the coast. People are jumpy, irritable."

He hadn't noticed, but just then a mother and father snapped at their two kids, who were complaining about carrying all their beach gear and a couple glared at each other over a folded-out map.

"Like that?"

Her hands fluttered about her face before she dropped them in her lap. "I'm worried. What if there's a copycat?"

"Why should there be? This is no serial killer like our math teacher."

"I feel it…something." She'd clenched her hand against her stomach. "Here."

He ruffled her hair. "You're on edge, too. Maybe you should relax."

"Do not suggest another massage. I don't want to lie naked on a table at someone's mercy."

He wiped his brow with the back of his hand. He needed a cold shower after that image slammed into his brain. "I was going to suggest you go up to your room, lock the doors and lie down with the drapes closed."

"And what will you be doing?"

He'd like to be lying next to her.

"I have an errand. In fact, can I borrow your car to pick up a package at the post office? From the description the hotel clerk gave me, it's too big for my bike."

She rubbed a circle on her left temple with two fingertips. "I'll drive you."

"You don't even trust me with your rental car?"

"You still have a lot of explaining to do." She stood up, facing him, and poked him in the chest.

His heart flipped. That meant she'd decided to allow his explanations. "It's a long story. I think I'll have to do it over lunch."

"I just had breakfast."

"I can wait." He traced a dark circle beneath her eye. "You still need to lie down and get some rest."

"I don't feel tired."

He knew better than to tell her she looked tired. "That's because you're wired. We're going to a concert tonight and we need to be alert."

"Okay. Let's get your package and go to bed." She sucked in a breath. "I mean, I'll go to bed. You can do whatever you want."

"They don't call them Freudian slips for nothing." He wrapped a lock of her hair around his finger. "You still need to get these crispy ends trimmed."

"That's the last thing on my mind."

"What *is* on your mind, Kylie?" Tugging on her hair, he drew her closer. "Did you get some kind of vibe from that roadie?"

"It's the whole morning. I'm out of sorts." She covered her ears. "I wish someone would turn off that car alarm."

"Mail, then rest." He steered her outside by lightly clasping her shoulders from behind. "Where'd you park?"

"Around the back. The hotel is getting crowded."

"More people in for the concert."

He followed her down the walkway on the side of the hotel, his thigh brushing against the fragrant jasmine that grew in a jumble in the planters.

The car alarm grew louder.

Turning to him, she wrinkled her nose. "Do you have your wallet and the notice to claim the package?"

He patted the back pocket of his jeans. "Right here. Why?"

"You look like you just rolled out of bed."

He combed his fingers through his short hair. "Yeah, because you weren't in your room. Woke me up real fast."

They waited for a car to pass before crossing the parking lot where her car faced a low brick wall. As they approached the rental, Kylie's steps quickened and Matt took longer strides to keep up.

"What's your hurry all of a sudden?"

"Don't you see it?" She skipped into a jog. "That's *my* alarm."

By the time they reached the car, he saw the sprinkles of glass on the asphalt. Then he saw the gaping hole in her window.

"Looks like someone smashed your window." All his muscles tightened. A broken window would be annoying, but given the threats to Kylie the past few days the jagged hole in the window gave off a more ominous air.

"Damn it." The quaver in her voice meant she felt it, too.

"You have your purse." He tugged at the strap over her shoulder. "It's just a broken window."

"Matt." She gripped his arm in an iron vise. "I—I left something in the front seat."

He yanked open the back door to unlock the front, and the rest of the glass cascaded to the ground. He flicked the lock and opened the front passenger door. The seat was empty. "It's gone. What was it?"

She turned to him, a look of dark dread in her eyes. "Bree's scarf. Someone stole Bree's scarf."

Chapter Fourteen

The sledgehammer in her head fell harder and she swayed against the car.

Matt tucked his arm around her waist and pulled her away from the glass.

"It's okay, Kylie. It's just a scarf." He whispered in her ear but it sounded like shouting.

The scarf. The scarf.

Pushing against his chest, she said, "I can't go on without the scarf. It was my link to Bree. Somebody knew that."

"What about Toby and Kenny? They were in your car. They probably took the scarf." He took the keys from her hand to start the engine and disengage the alarm.

"They took the scarf when I dropped them off at the concert grounds, and then came back here and broke the window of my car? That makes no sense at all."

He returned to her side. "Why would someone want Bree's scarf? To frighten you off? If an exploding house didn't do that, a missing scarf wouldn't."

Maybe Matt wanted to soothe her, to make light of the situation, but he had to realize the significance of this theft.

"Don't you get it?" She bunched his T-shirt in her hands. "Bree's killer took the scarf to throw me off."

Matt started shuffling pieces of glass into the dirt with the toe of his flip-flop. "You told me a personal item helped. You didn't say you needed it."

"I don't. I didn't." She flung open the car door and ran her hands across the seat as if the scarf had become invisible. She'd never had to rely on something that belonged to the victim for past cases. It did help, but she could do her job without it. But this case?

Working with Matt had scrambled her frequency. She couldn't concentrate. She couldn't focus on Bree. How was she going to get justice for that young woman?

Twisting her head over her shoulder, she took in Matt's expectant face. She didn't want to admit how much his presence had thrown her off her game. And making love with him last night?

Total mistake.

"It helps—a lot. I wanted the scarf for tonight, the first night of the festival."

"Maybe we can get you something else?"

"And admit to Mrs. Harris that I lost her daughter's scarf?" She turned and plopped on the seat of the car, wringing her hands in her lap.

"You didn't lose it. Someone stole it from you, the same someone who's been threatening you since you got here."

"Why am I the target? You're working on the case, too."

His lips twisted into a smile. "Maybe the killer knows I'm a failed cop and doesn't have much faith that I'm going to solve this thing. Hell, everyone else in town seems to know my business."

"And those jaunts to the post office for personal reasons? Do they have anything to do with your failure as a cop?"

"Yeah, they do. Confidential correspondence from my attorney. That's why the mail carrier couldn't leave it at the hotel." He snapped his fingers. "I still have a package to collect. Are you up for driving? I can drive myself."

"You're not on my rental agreement. I'd better drive."

He pointed to the broken window. "Are you going to report this to the police?"

"Might as well, but I doubt they're going to be concerned about a missing scarf."

"Maybe not, but they might be able to get some prints from the door."

Kylie agreed and they waited a half hour for the cops to come and lift prints from the door handle. They promised to rule out Kylie's and Matt's prints but Kylie wasn't going to hold her breath for the results.

When the cops left, Kylie drove to the post office and pulled the car to the curb across the street from the post office. "I'll wait here."

"Come in with me...humor me."

Sighing, Kylie pushed open her door. If she ever hoped to communicate with Bree, she had to get some alone time...away from Matt.

He took her hand and squeezed it as they crossed the street. This simple touch reminded her of everything they'd shared last night. No man had ever made her feel the way Matt had. Maybe it was all the practice he'd had, but even the thought of other women couldn't dampen the pleasure she'd felt from his experienced hands, mouth, tongue...

She ground her teeth together. How was she ever supposed to think about dead people when this man's vibrancy made her feel so alive?

He didn't release her hand until they both made it to the counter. Matt dug a slip of paper from his back pocket, along with his wallet. "I'm picking up a package."

He slid the notice toward the post office clerk. She glanced at it and asked for his ID. Then she turned and disappeared into the bowels of the back office.

While they waited, Matt tapped Kylie's nose. "You're still going to let me explain, aren't you? I'm sorry I kept the information from you. I just didn't want to put anything more on your plate."

Great. He was about to explain away the one barrier that might keep her from rushing headlong so far down a course, she'd never make her way back to the shore of sanity and reason. Or did she have that wrong? Did Matt represent that shore? A safe haven from the turmoil and despair that had driven her mother to take her own life?

She'd have to consider that, but for now she still had a case to solve. Closure to bring. Justice to serve.

A broken window to report to her car rental agency.

The clerk plunked a big, square box on top of the counter. "Here you go, Mr. Conner. Sign here."

"What's this?" Matt swept a thick, padded manila envelope from the top of the box.

"Apparently, that went to the hotel also, so they just sent it over with the box." She tore off the top of the triplicate form after Matt signed it.

"Thanks." Matt hoisted the box in his arms, which looked like it weighed two tons. As the envelope on top began to slip, he secured it with his chin. "Can you take that?"

Kylie snatched it and studied the front label, typed out to Matt in care of the hotel. His attorney hadn't bothered with a return address on this one. "More stuff from your attorney?"

"Probably. We just might win my case based on the amount of paperwork alone."

"So, you have a case?"

"I'm suing the department." He dumped the box into the trunk of her car. "I was set up to take the fall for a theft, Kylie."

THREE HOURS LATER, after Kylie reported her broken window to a bored car rental agent and Matt had dug through the box of papers from his attorney, they faced each other over sandwiches and a pitcher of iced tea. The waiter had just left the pitcher after they'd made it through three glasses each.

Matt dabbed his forehead with a napkin. "This has to be some record-breaking temperatures for the coast."

"It's hot." Kylie pressed her sweating glass against her cheek. "Did you find what you needed in that box…or the envelope?"

"I'm looking through some old drug cases."

"Were you a narcotics officer?"

"Yep, but I was looking into some irregularities in the department—facts and figures that weren't adding up."

"Someone got wind of you nosing around and turned the tables on you?"

"You're a quick study…and you didn't even need to use ESP to figure that out." He poured more tea into his glass and topped hers off, too.

"How'd they do it? How'd they set you up?"

Matt took a bite of his sandwich and chewed, staring past Kylie and out the window. This is where it got sticky. "They used a woman, a local reporter."

Kylie narrowed her eyes. "She was in on the setup?"

"Uh-huh." He dropped his sandwich onto his plate where it toppled over. "I started noticing discrepancies between reported drug busts and evidence storage. When I looked into it, it seemed as if certain records had been altered to match the money and drugs in storage."

"You're stalling, Conner. Where did the woman come into the picture?"

"She came to me. Spotted me in a cop hangout one night."

"A bar?"

"Where I was nursing my single beer." He took a sip of iced tea since the temperature had just increased another ten degrees. "I knew her from a few other drug busts that she'd covered. She told me she'd received an anonymous tip about the theft of drugs and money from the department. It dovetailed with what I'd been investigating."

"Why didn't you tell a superior?"

"I did, Kylie."

She blinked. "Your superior was in on the fix, too?"

"That's right." His hand crumpled the napkin in his lap. "Anyway, Mara, the reporter, gave me a tip on a big drug deal going down at a club. Our team organized a raid, and the next thing I knew, I was being accused of stealing money and drugs from the raid. The bust went badly, too—as if they were expecting us. A woman died in the crossfire and I got blamed for that, too."

"They set you up to shut you up and they used the reporter to nail you, so to speak."

He shoved his plate away, his appetite evaporating like a drop of water on the sizzling sidewalk. "She played her part flawlessly. Someone had been warning her to back off. She needed my help."

Kylie snorted and then dabbed her nose. "I'm sorry, but somebody in that department had your number and pushed all the right buttons."

"I was a real sap, a total pushover."

She ran her thumb along the knuckles of his fist clenched beside his plate. "You're one of the good guys, Matt. Apparently, you always have been. They played on that."

"My penchant for playing a superhero landed me on the street."

"If it hadn't been a woman in peril, it would've been something else. You were threatening them and they had to get you out."

She shrugged her shoulders in a careless gesture that told him she'd momentarily forgotten her worries from this morning. Instead of adding to her problems, his sorry tale had allowed her to shove her own into the background.

But she knew him better now. How would she have reacted if he'd told her from the beginning of their acquaintance?

He held out his hand. "Am I forgiven for keeping that from you?"

"Nothing to forgive." She clasped his hand. "I'm just wondering if part of your M.O. for making a woman feel safe and protected includes bedding her."

Ouch.

He disentangled his fingers from her surprisingly strong grip. "I didn't… That's not why…"

"Save it." She drew her finger across her lips. "I just want to find out what happened to Bree."

"In a weird coincidence, Harlan Sloan is part owner of the club we raided on that fateful day."

"Really? That is weird." She drummed her fingers on the table, the furrow returning between her eyebrows. "Now that we're being completely honest, how'd you get this job, anyway?"

"I'd just put out my shingle and Mr. Harris called me. I always figured my partner sent him my way because he knew I grew up here. How about you?"

"I live in Portland like the Harrises. The local paper ran a story on me, Mrs. Harris read it, saw that I was from Coral Cove and contacted me."

"You must be a big deal if newspapers are writing stories about you."

She rested her chin on her folded hands. "I've had my successes, but I'm afraid Mrs. Harris put her faith in the wrong medium."

"Don't sell yourself short, Kylie. You've had a lot of distractions. How can you concentrate on finding Bree when someone's trying to kill you?"

Her long lashes dropped over her eyes. "I have to get back on track somehow."

"The show starts tonight. Being there, in the same environment as Bree when she disappeared, has got to help." He yawned and covered his mouth with his fist. "What's our game plan for tonight?"

"Looks like you're the one who needs rest now."

"Well, we both had a late night, not that I minded in the least."

She pursed her luscious lips. "I think we need to stick to business."

The pleasant burning in his belly that had

started when he thought about rolling around in the sheets with her dissipated, and he cleared his throat. "Of course."

"I think you should get some sleep. I'm going to relax by the pool, order some room service for dinner and we can hit the opening act of the show together. How does that sound?"

"That sounds good." He waved at the waiter to get the check. "Can I join you for dinner in the room?"

"Sure."

As Matt paid the bill, he slid a sideways glance at Kylie, looking like a cat who'd just discovered the rat's hideout. After she'd announced her plan, he immediately had a hankering to relax poolside, but maybe he should continue to go through the cases Andy had sent him and let her have some alone time.

The pool, with its myriad families and kids splashing around, would be safe enough. He yawned again. And, man, he could use the sleep.

HOLDING HER BREATH, Kylie eased open the door between her room and Matt's. His large, shirtless frame was sprawled on the bed, piles of papers stacked around him and in neat rows on the floor. His chest rose and fell with each deep, slumbering breath.

She could drive out to the concert grounds before him and try a little meditation without his all-encompassing presence. She sucked in her bottom lip. She'd be safe among all those concertgoers. She'd leave Matt a note and they could meet up later.

The cell phone in her pocket buzzed and she stepped back from the adjoining door and slid it from her jeans.

I have something of Bree's TR.

Her pulse ticked up a few notches.

TR—Toby Reynolds. She'd seen him out at the pool and told him about the broken window and the missing scarf. He'd mentioned he might have something that belonged to Bree, something Mindy had shown him.

Her gaze darted to Matt's door and back to her phone. This was even better. If she could get an item of Bree's from Toby, she could get some serious work done before she met up with Matt. Then she'd really have something to contribute to this investigation.

She hit the Reply button on her phone and texted Toby that she'd meet him at the foot of the stage on the right-hand side.

Matt would go nuts again if she disappeared like this morning, so she grabbed a pad of paper with the hotel's logo on it and scribbled a note to him. She cracked open the door between their rooms, slipped the note in the doorjamb and pulled it closed, leaving it unlocked.

Placing her hands on the door, she said, "Sorry, Matt, but I have to do this alone."

She pulled her sweatshirt from the back of a chair and left her room, clicking the door behind her.

By the time she reached her car, her head was throbbing. She didn't mind the pain. It represented a disconnect from the land of the living to…that other place. And she needed to be in that other place to help Bree, or at least help her parents. Bree was beyond help now.

The line of cars turning off the highway meant the concert had begun. The heat of the day soaked into the night, and the air crackled with electricity. Had it been unseasonably hot three years ago?

Kylie followed the waving arm of the parking attendant. Sloan had gone all-out this year. Usually parking consisted of people abandoning their cars wherever they found a spot.

She pulled onto a thick carpet of pine needles next to a Jeep blaring music and laughter. Had Bree, Mindy and Patrice been as carefree that night? Now two of them were dead, and the third…

Kylie stumbled from her car and clutched her head. Music also resounded from the concert stage through the trees. Rockapalooza had come to life.

"Are you okay?" A teenager from the Jeep touched her shoulder.

She jerked her head up. "I'm okay. Just got a little dizzy."

"I heard there's a first-aid station...no questions asked. You know, if you get too loaded."

His female companions giggled while they hung their arms around each other and tramped off down the trail to the concert bowl.

Swell. Now she looked like another zonked-out concertgoer.

She put her aching head down and followed them. She had no intention of being alone tonight. Another group trouped down the path right behind her.

The path opened onto the concert bowl, teeming with color and movement. The first band had claimed the stage and the lead singer bellowed out some incomprehensible lyrics. Even if Kylie couldn't understand him, it resonated with the crowd, which cheered and surged en masse toward the stage.

The stage she had to get to.

Being solo and a woman didn't hurt her cause. She squeezed between knots of revelers, flashing a smile here and a loud *excuse me* there. At one point, her feet actually left the ground as one bunch made a rush toward the stage.

Her head pounded along with the drumbeat and

her fingertips tingled. She'd hit the zone. Now she just needed the means to get in touch with Bree.

Ten rows back from the action, she craned her neck to scan the security lined up along the edge of the stage. In a blue polo, Toby stood shoulder to shoulder with the other employees of Sloan Enterprises, the permanent security guys a bit beefier than the locals.

She ducked and shimmied between two guys jumping up and down, pumping their fists. A girl behind her yelled, "Hey, no creeping to the front," and plucked at Kylie's sweatshirt. Another body came between them, and the girl lost her grip.

The crush of the sweaty bodies increased Kylie's dizziness and sense of disorientation. *Is this how you felt, Bree?*

She staggered to the edge of the throng and then fell to her knees, the crowd spitting her out as if it were some giant, pulsating beast that had eaten its fill.

Gentle hands encircled her arms and she looked up into the angelic face of Toby Reynolds.

"I'm glad you made it, Kylie. I have something of Bree's."

MATT SHIFTED AND a sheaf of papers crinkled beneath his left arm. He coughed and rolled to his side, peering at the illuminated digits on the alarm clock. Another forty-five minutes and they'd be ready to go. They'd wanted to wait out the first couple of bands, get a bite to eat and avoid the opening-night traffic.

He pushed up to a sitting position and crunched the pillows behind his back. Rubbing one eye, he grabbed a stack of papers that represented one case. Andy had done his job. Matt had enough here to make a good case that the evidence room had all kinds of problems before the bust that ruined his career.

Turning, he grabbed a can of flat, warm soda and knocked the manila envelope that had come separate from the box to the floor. Drawing his brows over his nose, he picked it up.

Someone had typed up a neat address label, unlike Andy's messy scrawl across the box. Matt slid his thumb beneath the flap of the envelope and made a small tear. Pinching either side of the envelope he tugged it open. He puffed it out and peered inside.

Photos.

He shook the contents into his lap and tossed the envelope aside. Had Andy gotten hold of some incriminating photos? No note accompanied the pictures. He picked up the first one and studied the three smiling girls—Mindy, Patrice…and Bree.

Snatching the discarded envelope from the floor, he turned it over and squinted at the postmark. Someone had mailed it from Boston. The mysterious Patrice?

He plucked another picture out of the pile. This one showed the three young women with Eric, Kenny and Toby. They all looked…friendly. None of the guys had given the impression that they'd actually hung out with Bree.

He flipped through the stack and noticed a disturbing trend. In all of the pictures, Toby was positioned right next to Bree, always touching her, looking at her…gazing at her with longing.

He flicked the corner of one picture. Toby worked at the hotel, had access to the rooms. He'd known about Kylie's mother, had mentioned her by name. He was studying something scientific in college—chemistry? Wouldn't a chem student know how to rig an explosion like the one that rocked Rosie's house, or at least how to research it?

With his heart pumping, he swung his legs over the side of the bed, scattering more papers. Pinching a photo of Toby and Bree between his fingers, he charged toward the adjoining door and threw it open.

"Kylie?"

The neatly made up bed stared back at him blankly. His gaze darted to the bathroom door, slightly ajar. He stepped into the room and listened. No water running.

"Kylie?"

He stalked toward the bathroom and shoved open the door. One light glowed over the mirror in the empty room. He pounded the vanity, glaring at himself in the glass.

Where was she?

He walked back into the bedroom and slowly turned. She'd taken her purse, the sweatshirt that had hung on the back of the chair, her cell phone.

Cell phone.

He dug his own phone from his pocket, which fumbled out of his shaky hands. He stooped to pick it up and noticed a single white sheet of paper on the carpet. He grabbed it and read the note.

Matt, I went to the concert early. Some things I just need to do by myself. Don't worry. I'll text you a meeting place. Toby has something of Bree's.

Her bold signature in black ink blurred before his eyes.

He'd done it. The kid had lured her out with the promise of something she wanted more than anything. Something he'd taken from her in the first place—Bree's scarf.

He crushed the note in his fist and punched the button for Kylie's cell phone. It rang until her voice mail picked up.

Matt shouted into the phone. "Kylie, it's Toby. Get away from Toby."

Then he punched in the same text message.

He stormed into his own room, pulled on his boots and grabbed his leather jacket, his keys… and his Glock.

The roar from his motorcycle bellowed into the still night as he gunned the engine. He careened out of the hotel parking lot and hit the coastal highway at high speed.

Why did she do it? Why did she sneak away from him?

But he already knew the answer. She'd had to get away from his smothering presence. He was cramping her style, suffocating her. If he had given her more space, she wouldn't have felt compelled to escape…right into the arms of a killer.

Steady traffic still poured into the concert grounds, but he weaved between the cars with his bike. When he saw the turnoff to the venue, he shot ahead and rode on the shoulder of the road to pass the concertgoers.

The parking attendants waved him through and he cut the engine of his bike and walked it in as close to the bowl as he could. When he faced the clearing, now packed with bodies jumping up and down and swaying to the music, his gut twisted.

Where could she be in this teeming humanity?

Toby had shown him his blue polo shirt with a gold insignia for Sloan Enterprises Security. Security. He scanned the crowd and spotted a few blue polos.

He approached a beefy guy wearing one. "Hey, do you know Toby Reynolds? He's a townie."

The man hunched his shoulders. "Doesn't sound familiar, but most of the local kids are stationed up front, bordering the stage."

Matt tunneled his way through the crowd, pissing off more than a few people and stomping on a fair number of bare toes with his motorcycle boots.

He zeroed in on the blue shirts lining the stage, but couldn't see Toby or Kenny or even Rob. He grabbed another security guy by the sleeve and yanked him close to yell in his ear.

"Do you know Toby Reynolds?"

The guy shook him off, but nodded. "Yeah, I know him."

"Have you seen him around? Is he here?"

"He was here but I haven't seen him in a while." He turned back to the stage. "This band's about to wrap it up. Gotta get back to work."

Matt dragged a hand through his hair, and slumped against the corner of the stage. He pulled the photo of Toby and Bree from his pocket and traced the faces with his fingertip.

Where are you? Where did you take Bree? Where have you taken Kylie?

He combed through the snippets of conversation he'd exchanged with Toby. The guy had seemed bland—no wonder Bree hadn't been interested. He showed no emotion…except…Matt brought the photo close to his face. Columbella House loomed behind the couple.

He recalled when he'd mentioned tearing down Columbella to Toby. Fire had flashed from his usually vapid blue eyes. Now why would a young guy like that be so protective of an old house like Columbella?

Unless he had something to hide there.

Chapter Fifteen

Kylie stumbled over the threshold of a doorway, her legs numb and her brain foggy. A pair of strong hands gripped her from behind. Toby.

He had taken her here in his car, half dragged, half carried her because her limbs had turned to jelly. After…after…

Adrenaline coursed through her system and she jerked her arms against their restraint and widened her eyes. He'd shot her with something. She'd seen the needle…too late.

"Toby?"

The hands tightened their grip. "Coming around? Good. I didn't want you completely knocked out."

He whipped the cover from a chair and shoved her into it. Dust particles swirled in the beam of his flashlight and Kylie sneezed. When she opened her eyes, her gaze tracked around the room. Columbella House.

She concentrated on lifting her hand to wipe her nose, but it lay uselessly in her lap. She moved her tongue, forming words slowly. "What are we doing here?"

"Two things, really." He stepped back, folding his arms over his blue polo shirt. "I want you to tell my fortune. And I want to introduce you to Bree."

Goose bumps rushed up her arms, and Kylie clenched her muscles against the chill. "B-Bree's here?"

"Of course. I thought you were close to figuring that out because you kept coming here, and then I think finding Mindy's body confused you."

Three. Dead. Girls.

"Did you harm Mindy?"

"That stupid druggie? No." Toby placed the flashlight on the table next to Kylie and flexed his fingers, cracking his knuckles. "She always thought Harlan Sloan killed Bree. Just because he's rich and powerful doesn't mean he can do anything he wants. Mindy killed herself because she felt guilty about Bree. She and Bree had an argument before Bree left the concert."

Kylie breathed deeply through her nose. Whatever drug Toby had used on her seemed to be wearing off. "To meet you?"

"No." Toby lashed out with his fist, knocking over a candlestick on the shelf behind him. "She wouldn't leave the concert to meet me. I knew that. But she'd leave to meet Sloan."

"You sent that text message from Sloan's phone?"

"It was perfect. It lured Bree to me and it got Sloan in trouble later." He tilted his head and the light from the flashlight caught his blond hair. "You always have to lure them out with a promise of something they really want. Like you. But I didn't lie. I do have something of Bree's."

Kylie shivered, but she welcomed the sensation to her numb body. "You killed Bree because you were jealous?"

He narrowed his eyes and looked down his nose at her. "I killed her because she was too stupid to recognize what a slimeball Sloan was."

Finally able to raise her arms, Kylie folded them across her chest. She whispered. "Where is she?"

"We'll get to that later." He rubbed his hands together, and for the first time, Kylie noticed he had a knife sheathed at his belt loop. "First, I want you to tell my fortune."

She swallowed. Could she use Toby's *fortune,* as he called it, to get out of this? She could at least use it to waste time until Matt came to the rescue.

And how was he supposed to find her? Maybe someone at the concert saw her leave with Toby. She had no idea where Toby had left his car or how they'd gotten into Columbella House.

But she trusted Matt. Hadn't he always come through for her before?

Toby pulled a bottle of water from the backpack slung over one of his shoulders and thrust it at her. "It's clean. I want you fully aware so you can do my reading."

She raised a trembling hand and took the unopened bottle from him. She chugged half the contents before she came up for air. "Why are you so interested in your future?"

"I had my reading done before, you know." A mist floated across his blue eyes. "Rosie did it."

A knot tightened in Kylie's gut. Mom had given this weirdo, this killer, a reading?

"What did you learn?"

"She led me to Bree. She told me love would come into my life, someone special, but there would be an obstacle." The jaw of his baby face hardened.

Kylie licked her lips. "S-so why didn't you get rid of Harlan Sloan instead of Bree?"

"Sloan wasn't the obstacle." He blinked his eyes. "It was Bree herself. She was the obstacle. She didn't want me for anything more than a friend. I was tired of being a friend. I decided to keep her here with me in Coral Cove forever."

"Nothing lasts forever, Toby."

"Death does."

Her gaze dropped to the belt at Toby's waist. Could she lunge for it? Could she use it?

"Your mother told me to overcome the obstacle."

"I think she meant your own jealousy—that was the obstacle she saw."

"No!" He grabbed a handful of her hair and yanked it. Tears flooded her eyes. "That's not what she meant. Let's see if you're as good as your mother. That's why I was worried about you."

"You were worried about me?"

"When I heard you'd come to town to investigate Bree's disappearance, I was afraid you'd see everything as it happened. But you're not very good, are you?"

"I—I can't see everything as it happened."

His full lips twisted. "That's because you were too wrapped up in that P.I....that cop. He didn't concern me. I researched him. He's a thief and an opportunist. I figured he was just here for the money."

He's going to prove you wrong, Toby.

Toby unsheathed his knife and he thrust his other hand, palm up, under her nose. "What does my future hold?"

A prison cell or a loony bin.

She took his wrist and her skin crawled as she touched his soft flesh. She focused on the meaningless lines crisscrossing his palm. Her mother had always pretended to read palms, but really she went off the vibe from the person.

All Kylie could feel now was evil emanating from him. How had she missed it before? Toby was right about one thing—she'd been too wrapped up in Matt to get a clear vision of anything.

She cleared her throat. "I see that you're a good person, Toby. You've made mistakes, but you can correct them. You can make things right if you stop this now and turn yourself in to Chief Evans."

He snatched his hand away and smacked her across the face. She reeled back against the dusty chair, her cheek burning.

"You're a fraud. I probably never had to worry about you at all. You never would've found Bree, and you never would've known I was the one who ended her life."

Kylie rubbed her face. He'd slapped the side that she'd already scraped escaping the bomb blast— the bomb he had planted. She glanced down at the trace of blood on her fingertips. Hot anger surged through her veins, and she lunged for Toby's face, clawing him with her nails.

He stumbled back, warding her off with one arm and swinging his knife around with the other. He grazed her hip with the blade, just above the waistband of her jeans and inside her sweatshirt. She staggered under the pain, dropping one knee to the floor.

"Don't mess with me, Kylie. Bree messed with me and look what happened to her."

Gasping, Kylie clutched her side where she felt blood seeping through her T-shirt. "What did happen to her, Toby?"

"Glad you asked. Get up." He pinched her arm with his grip and yanked her to her feet. "We're going to find out right now."

He pushed her in front of him, and she could feel the point of the knife against her back. He propelled her up the stairs, right up to the third floor where her mother had hung herself. Had her mother seen through Toby? Had she felt like she hadn't done enough to save Bree?

They walked past the landing with its broken balustrade from Kylie's fall. Where Matt had saved her. *Felt like a million years ago.*

They continued down the hallway until they reached the end. Toby's eyes gleamed with excitement, and Kylie had an urge to delay what he had in store for her.

"The warning on my mirror?"

"I gave you a chance. If you had left then, none of this would be happening."

"The massage room?"

He shrugged. "A clumsy attempt, as were the lights on the stage, but that threw suspicion on Sloan, too, didn't it?"

"You rigged my mother's house?"

"Stop!" He banged his fist on the door at the end of the hallway. "I know what you're doing, but you can't avoid this, Kylie. And why would you want to? I'm giving you what you came here for."

He pulled open the door to what looked like a walk-in closet or storage area and pushed her in ahead of him. With his breath hot on her neck, he reached around her and started pressing on the wall at the back of the closet.

A panel clicked and he slid it open. "You wanted to locate Bree? Well, here she is."

Kylie covered her mouth with both hands and her knees buckled as she stared into the face of a grinning skeleton.

MATT SLIPPED THROUGH the side door, sweat dripping from his brow. His cop instincts had to be right—they hadn't failed him yet—not when he'd suspected something fishy in the drug evidence lockup and not when he'd suspected Chief Evans had something to hide with the police report. If the chief had only trusted his son more, maybe he would've nailed Toby three years ago.

It had to be Toby.

He had to be here…and Bree had to be here, too. *Three. Dead. Girls.*

Matt cocked his head listening to…silence. With

all the nooks and crannies in this house, that didn't mean a thing. He leaned against the kitchen wall and pulled off one boot. If Toby was holding Kylie somewhere in this house, Matt didn't need to announce his presence. He pulled off the second boot and set it next to the first one.

Kylie was smart enough to hold Toby at bay. He'd brought her here for a reason. Otherwise, he would've finished her off in an easier way. Matt ground his teeth together. If that killer harmed Kylie, he'd pay…big-time.

On his stocking feet, Matt crept into the hallway. He edged toward the library and peered into the burnt-out room. Just in case. The light from his flashlight scanned the scorched walls.

He backed up and did a quick reconnaissance of the rest of the first floor. His gaze flicked to the door that led to the basement. He reached out, his fingers grazing the handle. Then he heard a scream and a thump from upstairs.

He spun around and took the stairs, two at a time, all thoughts of a stealth attack banished by that scream—Kylie's scream. He hit the second floor, but the scrambling from above told him all the action was on the third.

He stormed the next set of stairs and crashed to a halt when confronted with Toby, his arm around Kylie's waist and a knife to her throat.

"Matt!" Kylie jerked in Reynolds's grip.

"How'd you find us? How'd you know?" Reynolds's knife gleamed in the light Matt had turned on him.

"Give it up, Reynolds. I called the police. They're on their way."

If only he'd done that. He couldn't get any reception on his cell at the concert venue and by the time he'd driven out of there, he'd been too anxious to reach Kylie to bother to make a call to the C.C.P.D. and try to explain to them how and why he knew Toby had Kylie in his clutches.

Was that really it? Had his desire to be Kylie's one and only savior put her life on the line?

Toby tightened his hold on Kylie, but his gaze darted past Matt's shoulders to the third-floor landing. "I don't care if they're on their way. That's not going to change what I have to do."

Matt took a step forward. "Sure it does, Toby. You wanted to…hurt Kylie because you were afraid she'd find out what you did to Bree, to keep what you did to Bree a secret. That's all over now."

Toby's face crumpled, and then he smiled. "But if the cops aren't on their way, nobody needs to find out. I'll take care of both of you."

Planting his feet in a wide stance, Matt expanded his chest and straightened to his full height. "You really think you can take me on, Reynolds?"

Toby waved the knife. "As soon as you toss your gun on the floor between us. I'm not dumb enough to bring a knife to a gunfight."

"Who says I have a gun?" Matt spread his arms wide.

"You're a cop…a former cop…you have a gun. Now throw it over the railing or I end it right here." He drew the knife across Kylie's throat.

"Don't do it, Matt. Don't put yourself at his mercy. He's crazy. What he did to Bree…"

Toby socked Kylie in the stomach and she coughed.

A muscle ticked in Matt's jaw. He'd kill the SOB.

"Do it, Conner. Toss the gun."

Matt pulled his weapon from the pocket of his jacket, checked the safety and tossed it where it clattered to the tile floor three stories down. He didn't need a gun to take down this loser.

"What did you do with Bree?"

Toby stepped to the side, dragging Kylie with him. "Come closer."

Matt took a few more steps toward Toby and Kylie.

Kylie whimpered. "She's behind a panel in the closet, Matt. He hung her by her wrists. She's been here for three years."

Three. Dead. Girls.

Mindy, Bree and Marissa St. Regis?

It must've driven Reynolds crazy…or crazier… that he hadn't been able to tell anyone about his handiwork all these years. That's why he hadn't killed Kylie on the spot, or why he didn't kill her right now. He needed to show off. He needed to bask in the glory of his cleverness.

Matt was all for basking, especially if it allowed him to get closer to Kylie.

"All this time, Reynolds?" He inched closer still. "That's amazing. How'd you know about that secret panel?"

"I've done my share of exploring around this house. Except in the basement." His blue eyes clouded over. "I won't go in the basement."

Matt balanced on the ball of his front foot, his hands splayed and ready at his sides. "I can't see her. I can't see Bree. I want to see what you've done."

Toby shuffled to his left. "You can take a closer look. She's in the back of the closet. The panel's open…for the first time in three years."

Training his gaze toward the closet, Matt sidled past Toby. When he drew level with him and Kylie, he shouted, "Duck, Kylie," and threw out an elbow to the side.

His blow cracked Toby on the cheekbone and he screamed. Kylie wriggled from Toby's grasp, as he blindly lashed out at her. She fell to the floor and scrambled away from him on her hands and knees.

Wielding the knife with his arms flailing, Toby charged Matt. Matt landed a punch against the angelic face and a roundhouse kick to Toby's midsection.

Toby grunted and staggered back, hitting the railing on the landing. The same one Kylie had fallen through days ago.

He flapped his arms in the air like some giant bird and then flung himself backward. The sickening crack that followed his fall told Matt all he needed to know.

Kylie was safe.

THE WARM WATER BUBBLED from the Jacuzzi jets, hitting Kylie right between the shoulder blades. She'd take this over a massage any day, especially given the view.

Matt smiled across from her as she walked her toes up his shin. "I can't believe you figured out Toby killed Bree from a photo, and then figured out where he'd taken me from a few offhand comments he made."

He tapped the side of his head. "Old-fashioned police work and observation."

"I guess it trumps my methods since I walked willingly into Toby's trap."

"You were fixated on getting something else

that belonged to Bree…and your whole mojo was off." He grasped her foot in his big hand and caressed her instep with his thumb.

She wiggled her toes. "Yeah, I had a different kind of mojo going on."

"Toby scrawled the warning on your mirror? He slipped into the massage room?"

"He was responsible for everything—the lights, the explosion at the house."

"But not Mindy."

"Chief Evans told me Mindy's death clearly pointed to suicide. Just like my mom's."

"You knew Bree was in that house, Kylie. You just got confused because Mindy's body was there, too."

"And Marissa St. Regis?"

"I have no idea where you got that, do you?"

She cupped a puddle of hot water in her palm and dumped it over the side. "Marissa did not just run away, Matt. She came to some harm in that house—I'm sure of it."

"Are you in touch with Mia St. Regis?"

"Not exactly, but I know how to contact her."

"Are you going to contact her?"

"Of course."

"Are you going to offer your services?"

"No. I need to get away from here, from all the memories."

His rough hand crept up her calf, and he brushed the back of her knee. "All the memories?"

"Memories of my mom."

"And me?"

The hot tub got hotter, and Kylie hoisted herself into the cool air. "All my memories of you are…good."

"My memories of you are—" his fingertips switched to the inside of her thigh "—better."

Her lips parted and her eyelashes fluttered as he leaned forward, the steam rising from his body. He kissed her mouth and then floated next to her onto the step.

"What are your plans, Matt?"

"You mean right this minute?"

She splashed him. "For the future."

"The documentation my attorney sent me looks good, Kylie." He took her by the shoulders and turned her toward him. "I'm going to fight for my job, and then I'm going to fight for you."

She sighed and rested her forehead against his broad chest. "I surrender."

"What?"

Raising her chin, she touched her nose to his, staring into his deep, dark eyes. "I said, I surrender. You don't have to fight for me. I'm yours. I've been yours ever since you pulled me from that third-floor landing at Columbella."

He kissed her again, pulling her flush against his chest. "Well, that was easy."

She smiled against his lips, feeling the warm presence of her mother floating above them in the steam.

"It was fate."

* * * * *

Don't miss the exciting conclusion of
Carol Ericson's miniseries,
GUARDIANS OF CORAL COVE.
Look for DECEPTION, on sale next month
wherever Harlequin Intrigue books are sold!

LARGER-PRINT BOOKS!
GET 2 FREE LARGER-PRINT NOVELS PLUS
2 FREE GIFTS!

Harlequin®

INTRIGUE®

BREATHTAKING ROMANTIC SUSPENSE